ERADICATOR

Apocalypse Party

Cover Design by Matthew Revert
Typesetting by Mike Corrao

Paperback: 978-1-954899-37-7

ERADICATOR

DAVID SIMMONS

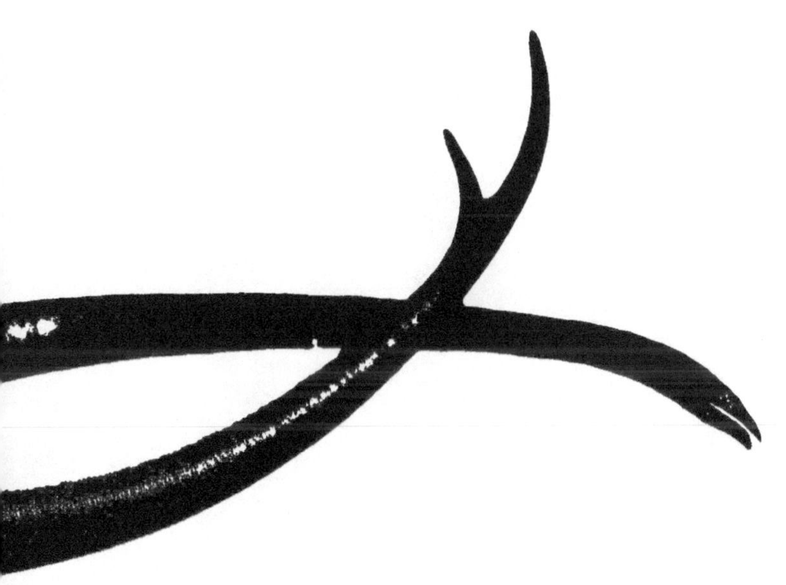

APOCALYPSE PARTY

For my daughters

I JUST FUCKING KILLED SOMEONE LOL. I STRANGLED THEM AND SLIT THEIR THROAT AND STABBED THEM NOW THEY'RE DEAD. I DON'T KNOW HOW TO FEEL ATM. IT WAS AHMAZ-ING. AS SOON AS YOU GET OVER THE "OHMYGAWD, I CAN'T DO THIS" FEELING, IT'S PRETTY ENJOYABLE.

— FROM THE DIARY OF ALYSSA BUSTAMANTE, RECOVERED BY THE COLE COUNTY SHERIFF'S DEPARTMENT IN OCTOBER, 2019

PART I
THORAX

CHAPTER 1

When it hits you, it's like a 50 caliber BMG to your solar plexus. It's like being crushed with a 140-ton hydraulic press. It's like endometriosis. Like broken glass in the core of you, and it just takes everything.

I dry swallow a Klonopin but it gets caught in the back of my throat. It's like bitter sandpaper. It's like yellow chalk. I gulp and I gulp, making deep-throating duck noises until I get it down. On the way to Euphoria, I see a man with no shirt being handcuffed on the hood of an unmarked Ford Explorer. His sweaty bald head is covered in thick scars, shiny keloid skin that slithers around his skull like nightcrawlers. A woman is standing outside in a pink velour Baby Phat sweatsuit, talking to a second police officer, metal clips in her still-setting hair. The police presses the man's face into the SUV windshield and he's trying to turn around and say something to the woman. He's yelling what sounds like, "You played, shordie, goddamn, you played like I ain't got a—" but our Uber driver blows the red light at Orleans and Patterson Park so I never get to hear the rest.

I shake another Klonopin out of the neon orange pill bottle and dry swallow it. The ulcers in my stomach smile like wounds.

Daneen's staring at me like I'm an abjection. "You really gotta get that looked at," she says, patting my tummy. Her fingertips leave an electric sizzle on the bare skin of my midsection. Pops and bursts of thermodynamic energy turn to blue ache and I'm turning away from Daneen and looking back out the window and wondering what that man was going to say.

"I can't believe I paid $50 for this pass," I tell her, and I mean it too. $50 gone and that doesn't include my outfit, my lashes, my hair, my wax, my eyebrows.

We work at Hopkins but that doesn't mean shit. Our insurance is terrible—it's the same for us as anybody else. I wedge my thumb in between my leggings and panties and use the knuckle of it to massage where I think one of my kidneys might be. The pain is like my veins are pumping hydrochloric acid. Like my marrow is molten. Like I'm a nerve. A magnesium flash bulb.

I check my Instagram, then press the heart icon in the upper right-hand corner. It tells me that Damien Thompson and others have liked my story. It tells me that my last reel has 433 likes. The video is just me in my car, rapping along with Sexyy Red. I close the app and open Facebook. Click the notification bell in the bottom right-hand corner of the screen. It tells me that Viola Lyles and others have reacted to my story and I can see Viola's profile image with a heart at the bottom. I think she might be one of my aunts, I don't know.

We make it to Euphoria right when my pill starts to kick in. The driver shouts something at us in an effeminate voice, something about five stars, and I float to a line that centipedes around the block, Daneen at my side, our hips locked together, walking in sync like we're choreographed and it's giving long legs like Rebecca Lobo.

The pill Daneen gave me before we got in the Uber—not my Klonopin prescription—must have been 3-MMC or some other designer drug because I feel like shit but I'm *really* feeling myself. Like, my insides are a sea lion getting thrashed around by tiger sharks, and yet, I know I look great and I've got this MDMA-like stimulation thing going on but with *none* of the empathy. We inch forward in line. My lungs feel heavy. Breathless, I turn my head from side to side and lap at the air. Electric eels snap at my sinuses and I'm crunching down on my teeth, really working my jaw. I search for a pencil or an ice cream stick to chew on and remember that the leggings I'm wearing have no pockets.

I check my phone again. Open Instagram. Go to Daneen's page, look at her last pic. It has over two thousand likes already. It's a picture of her toes after a pedicure with the caption "City Girls Up." It's not even a picture of her feet, just her glossy toes and skin that always looks wet and feverish.

But she posted that pic earlier this morning. I posted *my* reel on the way home from work today. Technically, her toe pic only has this many likes because she posted it so long ago. Hours before I even thought about posting a Sexyy Red car video.

The bouncer runs his wand along my body and when it touches my stomach I want to vomit black blood in his face like that dinosaur from Jurassic Park. He runs his wand up and down my legs and he hovers too long on my ass and something bursts inside of me. Black blood in the stool comes from a problem in the upper digestive tract. Red blood in your shit is from a problem somewhere lower, like your colon or your asshole itself. The pill starts hitting me hard, real hard, and I'm ready to give this man my all when Daneen gets my arm in an elbow lock and brings me inside the club.

You have to go down a really steep incline to get into Euphoria so we tumble down the stairs like baby antelopes learning to walk and fall through the first door.

The hostess bats her fake eyelashes and ignores us.

"We have passes," Daneen says, but she lets the end of the word *passes* climb upwards a bit, like she's asking a question, in that condescending way that people with Daneen's upbringing have a tendency to do. She lays the glossy passes on the counter.

The hostess doesn't take them. "They no good."

"Huh?" Daneen asks. "What do you mean they're no good? I bought them online today. For tonight!"

The hostess doesn't look at the passes when she slides them back to Daneen. "What I said. These are for standard entry. Tonight's a premium situation. Big Poliano's performing. You not hip? You ain't see the flyer, girl?"

Daneen seethes. "Of course I *saw* the flyer. That's why I bought the passes. For the event on the flyer."

"Well," the hostess shrugs, bats her ridiculous eyelashes, "like I said, they no good."

"Fuck it," Daneen says to me, rummaging in her MCM clutch. "I'll take care of it."

Daneen always takes care of it.

She hands the hostess some money and we make our way inside Euphoria. It's all neon green strobes and post-coital sweat effluvium from the moment we step foot in the main section.

"You know anybody with a table tonight?" Daneen asks.

I shake my head.

Daneen arches her back, holds her hands up like claws and hisses like a startled cat. "Nobody?"

It feels like a mosquito is crawling on my abdomen, but on the inside surface of my skin. I rub and I rub and it does nothing. I'm too high. There's no way I can sit down at a table of nameless, smooth-faced men and pretend to be interested in them or what they're saying or what they do. I just can't do it tonight.

"I'm telling you, Jada, you look sick as fuck."

"I'm fine," I tell her, "I'm just peaking."

Daneen frowns. "Huh?"

My eyes do the nystagmus thing, bouncing back and forth at light speed horizontally, glassy orbs racked in the sockets and rolling around in my skull like billiards.

"I don't feel shit, Jada," and when she says my name, she says the "*da*" like "*duh*," and for this infraction I want to kill her. For this slight, I want to butcher my best friend and I want it to hurt and last forever and cause dysfunction in the lives of her loved ones. I want her death to be confusing for her perfect fucking family. "I'm just saying," she continues, "I took the same bullshit as you and I don't feel anything."

"Really?" I don't even want to kill her anymore. I'm more interested in why she doesn't feel these pills we both took.

Daneen ignores me and elbow locks me again, escorts me like a child. I black out for a moment and we end up in a section with some of those nameless, faceless men but at least I can sit down. I kick off my platform pumps, toe them under the circular glass table and grab a bottle of Casamigos from the ice bucket on top of it.

"Oh shit," one of them says. "Your friend came to turn up, for real. That's what's up."

He clinks a glass of something brown with his friends. Daneen twerks and sticks her tongue out the side of her mouth and says, "Owwwwwww."

Her teeth are so white, almost phosphorescent in the kaleidoscope lighting.

Looking around at the bodies. Throngs of flesh. Writhing torsos. Shiny meat. The smell of sweat and fruit. They dance in the style of "rub your body up and down, starting with your breasts; stick your tongue out; bend over and twerk; repeat." It's all the same dance and of course I usually do it too.

Just not tonight.

One of the men—I'm not sure which one, it could be the first one who spoke, the other, others, I'm not even sure how many of them there are right now in the section—scoots over on the couch in my direction. He's wearing an $800 Amiri shirt. "So, y'all, like, work together?" he asks, the stupid piece of shit.

At this point, Daneen must have already told him and his friends that we work at the hospital together or else why the fuck would he ask that? And if he knows that already, which he does, why the fuck would he ask that?

I want to tell him that on my morning commute from Rosedale, I drive with a backseat full of white fence pickets, stacked in rows of five and wrapped in twine. There are thirty pieces of fencing. Exactly fifteen of the pickets are three feet in length, while the remaining pieces are only two.

I want to tell him that I pull over on the Pulaski Highway around North Haven or North Highland and park my car in the shoulder lane. I put my hazards on. I carefully select one three-foot picket, as

well as one two-footer. I have my toolkit: a leather mat that I roll up which contains flowers, one hammer, one sharpie and one box of nails—the only tools I need for this venture.

I lay one of the long pickets out and hammer the shorter piece across the upper half of it, perpendicular like. I hold it up, two-handed.

A white cross.

A three foot, white picket cross that I bury in the ground along the side of the highway. I take out the sharpie and write a name across the horizontal part of the cross. The name doesn't matter.

I throw the flowers at the base of the cross.

The cars rush by and the wind screams across the highway, blowing my hair in every direction.

I get back in my car, turn off my hazards and pull onto the road.

"You good?" Amiri Shirt is asking me if I'm OK with what I assume is a look of concern, but I can never know.

"Yeah, you fucking piece of shit," I seethe. My foundation has started to melt, dripping to my chin so that I can feel it create a string of beads on my jawline, so I pour myself another glass of Casamigos.

"What? What did you just say?"

He backs up a bit.

"I said, I'm good," I tell him, edging closer. "I asked you if I could sit on your lap. And you're over here asking me if I'm OK and shit. Asking me to repeat myself when I'm just trying to have a good time."

I don't know why I'm doing it. I hate the faceless bag of meat and it feels like a Xenomorph is about to burst from my chest but I have to do something or I'm going to chew my molars down to nubs. I feel his heartbeat slow. I smell him relax. I get on top of him. I sit so my ass is in his crotch and my legs are together, calves and ankles touching. I grind on his dick with disinterest and think about killing people I've never met. He gets hard but it's like his erection knows I'm not putting my all into this.

Euphoria is a foul black rookery.

The men all turn to vultures and Daneen is now a vulture and I have to understand that I am one too. I flap my wings against the others. For a moment, we take flight as one. The skies darken. A swarm of scavengers, our massive wingspans blotting out the sun.

We land as one.

All of us, jostling for space on the few remaining perches. Fighting for cramped scraps of ground. Fighting over meager scraps of carrion. Snarling, snapping, frenzied feeding. Broken eggs and shattered fragments of bone. Beaks snapping. Beating our wings against the ashen, paper sky.

And then I'm back.

With this fuck asking me if I'm a CNA or an RNA.

I tell him, "If you ever get hurt really badly, and they have to take you to Hopkins, you'll find out," and I say it in a flirtatious way as I gyrate on his dick, and I even add a coy little giggle after the word *out* for the razzle dazzle, but I feel him tense up and then he's flaccid. This isn't true. I am a child passenger safety technician. I'm part of the life-giving process, not the life-saving process. But it's a fun line, a clever one. I feel him kind of withdraw from me a bit. He removes his hands from my waist. It must be too late for seductive threats.

CHAPTER 2

Listen, this is how attractive I am: if we are dating, and I decide to show up at your job with lunch, or simply to tell you hello, after I leave, your female coworkers will take you aside and compliment *you* on how beautiful *I* am, and they will do it with wide eyes and bewildered expressions, not because they don't think you're good enough for me, but because they see me and think that I'm too good for anyone. Someone called it *unattainable* beauty. I call it the type of look that can make you do things.

It's also the type of look that makes other people want to do things for you, if that's what I desire. Back to your female coworkers. Now they want to fuck you. They're attracted to you now because they think you have something special. Because I want you, they must want you.

This is how attractive I am.

I have weaponized my features, sharpened myself on the wheel of the city. This is what I look like:

I am more than an attractive being, I am beautiful as an inanimate object. I am a sunset. My vibrant colors are linked to evolution. But at the same time, I can hurt too.

I am a person and I have feelings.

Sometimes my feelings get so big that I can't keep them inside and I go to work with Dr. Marcic and Xiomara and Daneen and the nurses whose names I don't know and when they ask me how I'm doing, instead of just saying *fine, thank you*, I tell them about a movie I watched over the weekend that really touched me, the one where the irresponsible man-child has to figure out how to be a good single dad because his wife dies from a pulmonary

embolism while giving birth to their daughter, but then I notice they aren't nodding or making eye contact with me, or reiterating what I'm saying back to me in a reflective listening sort of way, and their words of affirmation are things like *oh wow* and *that's crazy*, so I know they're not paying attention to me at all and it makes me feel *so* invisible.

Like I'm nothing.

Then I wish I never said anything at all. Then I wish I was dead and I hate myself for feeling sorry for myself and I have trouble sleeping because I keep replaying the interaction over and over again in my head, so I order sheets from Sferra, the real Giza cotton, the highest quality grade with the forty millimeter fibers, not the fake shit that just *says* Egyptian cotton but really isn't, and then I remember that I am a beautiful flower. I am the fragility and sheer awe of nature, of life itself. Where flowers grow, life can thrive. You can grow, you can thrive. I am a Bugatti Veyron. I give you the power to move faster than everyone else. I'm engineered to be this way, with shapes and facets and symmetries and patterns you can't resist. You like my symmetry because healthy humans are symmetrical. You find me beautiful because my beauty ensures your survival.

I am knives-that-aren't-knives.

This is how sad I get sometimes: my insides start to ache with a blue cold, deep down in the core of me and it looks something like this:

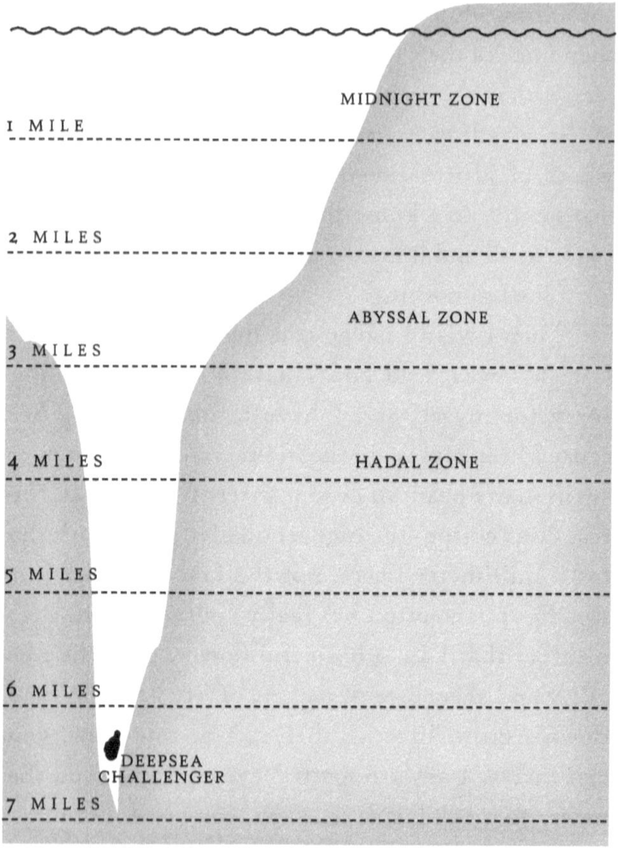

What I'm saying is that I feel like the Challenger Deep at the bottom of the Mariana Trench, which is the lowest part of the ocean floor known to man, so that's pretty low. I feel like my stomach is spread across the seabed. It feels so bad sometimes. I pop a Klonopin or crush an Oxy in the bathroom and blow it, but it still doesn't make the ache stop. It's such a dull, boring ache. This is different from the physical pain. This is different from the changes happening inside of me.

CHAPTER 3

SOMEHOW, I GET HIM BACK TO MY GARDEN APARTment in Rosedale and neither of us really know how we got there. He's too drunk. Me, I'm fucked up off that pill that Daneen said was a dud and my usual rounds of Klonopin and whatever is going wrong with my insides that keeps making me black out.

Where is Daneen?

And it's not even blacking out really. I'm still there. I just can't see shit. And I can't really do shit, or, well, I can do shit, but I'm not the one in control when I'm doing it. Whatever that means.

The TV is on because I left it that way. I don't like it when it's too quiet in my apartment. I scroll with the Firestick remote, try to find something to put on, music videos or just music, something, even old *Law and Order: SVU* reruns will suffice.

I come to the local news, where the thumbnail preview image is what appears to be a CCTV screenshot of an individual in a gimp suit brandishing an absurdly large shotgun. I click OK.

The thumbnail image dissolves and is replaced with a full screen image of a black woman with a dyed-blond caesar cut who looks like Fantasia. She says:

"Just moments before police believe Baltimore police reform activist Paratma Gleesh was killed, surveillance footage captured her alleged attackers following her into the elevator of her apartment on Lime electric scooters, like the ones found all over the city that can be rented via mobile app. We want to warn you, some of our viewers might find the following images disturbing."

The CCTV footage shows three gimp-suited individuals on electric scooters chasing a woman through the lobby of a building. One of the gimps wields a shotgun, the other two with bicycle chains that they helicopter above their heads.

The reporter continues:

"The footage sheds light on an alleged Saturday night interaction between Gleesh and her ex-boyfriend. Up until now, Gleesh's ex-boyfriend had been a suspect, but in light of this recently discovered evidence, the BPD plans to release him."

I turn the volume on the Firestick up and approach Amiri Shirt. I ask him if he needs a condom or if I need to get one and I never hear his answer because it doesn't matter. I sit him on my imitation Vladamir Kagan serpentine sofa and pull his track pants down around his ankles. I try to get his boxers down but he fights me a little, raising up on the couch, pulling away into the cushion.

"Hey," he says. Nervous laughter. A wide-nostril inhale of restored confidence that I hear, but do not see, because he has no face. "I'm fucked up."

"Me too," I tell him, reaching into the opening in his boxers and caging his balls. He shivers. His dick hangs timidly, small and withered when it brushes my knuckles. It smells sour and a spider's web strand of pre-cum slug trails my index to middle finger.

My stomach starts hurting so bad that I almost can't do it. I double over and clutch at my side.

"Hey," he says, reaching out to me. "We don't have to do this. We don't have to do anything. We can just chill or whatever. Just let me—"

I sit up and press my palm against his chest, pushing him back into the couch. "Don't go. Just give me a second."

I get up and head to the bathroom, losing my clothing as I go, making sure he sees my tits move when I take my shirt off facing away from him.

Under the sink is where I keep a really big knife. It's not a special knife or anything. When I showed it to Daneen, she told me it wasn't a knife.

"That's not a knife," she said, looking at me like I was a stain. "That's a machete."

Daneen is the only human person I've ever shown my knife to, so if she says it's a machete then it must be. Daneen is probably the only person I've ever loved. What do I know about knives anyway? I spent that night on my phone going down a machete rabbit hole. There's Barongs and Billhooks

and Bolos and Bowies and Colimas and Kukris. All kinds of these things. I researched machetes until I fell asleep without putting my phone on the charger and I'm *still* not entirely sure which one mine is.

I don't know if mine is a Parang or a Panga when I step behind the sofa and saw off the head of the man that's sitting on it. It's easier this time because he's so drunk. He reaches for his neck and I take a few of his fingers. He lets go of the blade and sticks his arms out straight like he's about to stand up and do a jumping jack, unsure what to do next. He's so confused. He's so surprised.

He passes out, face smooth, before I can get through the thyroid cartilage. He dies, stupidly, before I ding the blade on his hyoid bone.

CHAPTER 4

I WAKE UP SMELLING LIKE SEX ALTHOUGH I HAD none. Amiri Shirt in the living room has yet to begin his transformation, so the air is still crisp with whiffs of copper and wet car battery. My apartment is a one-bedroom, income-based housing situation in Rosedale, which is not the most pleasant place, but that's only if you're being negative, and being negative is the first step on the road to becoming a bitter bitch.

It's giving jaded.

It's giving hater.

My kitchen is small with an L-shaped Formica countertop that bends at the corner and is the only thing separating the dining room/living room from the kitchen but, really, this is not so bad, because I have stuck with the recommendation of *Architectural Digest*'s January 2018 issue and implemented bold, monochromatic colors, creating intentional cohesion.

The thing is, when you work with a monochromatic color palette, the soul of the space becomes the focus, rather than the trappings inside of it.

But I do have trappings. I have an imitation Schwartz lamp from Temu in the corner of my living room behind my 65-inch television, also from Temu. The lampshade is of a burnt wood variety, ebony. It's smoky black. It symbolizes depth and timeless elegance.

I am elegant and timeless.

And people think going monochromatic is low maintenance, because it's *less than*, but similar to a short cut hairstyle, it takes a lot of investment. Straying from a myriad of shades and hues can be quite intimidating when you actually try to do it.

Because I make less than $38,000 annually, I qualify for what I think is a pretty nice place that only costs me $700 per month to rent, utilities included. Because I pay so little on rent, I can buy myself nice things. Treat yourself, don't cheat yourself, is what I say.

Sometimes I get sad thinking about all the people I won't get to hurt before they stop me.

The centerpiece of my living room is the couch—the replica Vladamir Kagan serpentine sofa where Amiri Shirt sits, as previously mentioned—in a fleshy mauve tone. Armless and S-shaped, not designed for pushing up against a wall. Like a swoosh, or a squiggle of plush modernism. A biomorphic shape, like in nature.

I love it because it looks like an organ.

At Hopkins I don't get to look at organs but it makes me wet anyway—the *knowing* that they're nearby, opened and exposed. When I am at work, I fantasize about laparoscopic surgeries and touch my-self in between patients. I like those the best, the lap-aroscopic ones. This is because they blow up the torso like a big balloon to do it. Inflating people is silly.

I think about the patient I had last week, the one who had just given birth to twin girls and asked me to come closer so she could hiss in my ear that she was living in hell. I think about the 22-week mi-cropreemies in their fish tanks, tubes coming out of their bodies, perturbed expressions on their mal-formed faces. I think about the father who passed out when Xiomara asked if he wanted to hold his dying infant.

And then I cum.

You can get over almost anything except losing a child.

CHAPTER 5

ARLINGTON FAWOLE IN HR ASKED ME TO COME in so I'm here, sitting in his office, with him and his disgusting, bulbous, spider's egg sac-stomach that hangs over his belt in a sexual kind of way.

I take out my phone and check Instagram. The number "34" in a red circle in the corner of the app icon. Thirty-four notifications.

"Here's how it's gonna go," he says.

"Here's how it's gonna go?" I raise my voice a little. This is not starting off well.

"Jada," he says, making a pyramid with his hands on his desk like a fucking pussy. "This isn't the first time we've gotten a complaint from somebody about your behavior. At this point, we have to look at it as a pattern of sorts."

I let out a sigh and place my chin on my fists like a reprimanded child. "Who complained?"

"That's not the point."

"It was Phil."

"I can't—"

"Fuck Phil." I cross my arms *and* my legs defiantly.

"This is what I'm talking about."

"So, Phil said I said *fuck him*?" I ask.

Arlington shakes his head. "No. I never said it was Phil. I'm just saying that—"

"So it wasn't Phil?"

"Listen," he says, turning towards his desktop monitor. "I'm going to read this. This is a grievance filed by one of your coworkers."

"OK, let's go," I say.

"'I asked Jada if she had completed her car seat compliance checklist with the patient in room 312,'" he reads from the monitor, the screen making blue and white squares on his eyeglass lenses. "'I wanted to make sure she was finished with her duties so I could ask the patient if she wanted to see a lactation consultant. Jada responded by asking me if I knew that the male deep-sea anglerfish was a fraction of the size of the female anglerfish, and that it doesn't share the bright bioluminescence or fearsome appearance of its female mate, and that it latches on to the females like a parasitic growth, and then...'"

"And then?" I press Arlington. "Go on."

It's giving confrontational eyebrows.

It's giving audible bruxism.

The Human Resource Coordinator sighs. "'...like a parasitic growth, and then it shoots its cum into the female, over and over again, until it dies. Just shooting its cum until it's dried up. Nothing but a dried up husk. Completely devoid of cum. Empty of all life.'"

I sit back and twirl my locs like I do when I think I'm cute, which is all the time. "So it *was* Phil."

"Not the point," moans Arlington.

"Fucking Phil."

He sits back and we're both sitting back, staring at each other like old enemies. Arlington Fawole is an Igbo Nigerian man, and he lives in Crofton. I know this because I have stalked him from LinkedIn to Facebook behind the veneer of fake profile pages of women with natural hair. No trace of a Nigerian accent can be heard when Arlington speaks, but he doesn't have a Baltimore one either, no shades of Maryland, as if he chose his own accent out of a catalog. His hair is closely cropped to his skull, and he wears gold Silhouette rimless eyeglasses. He has blue-light protection, so when he moves his head slightly, the lenses flash metallic sapphire with the fluorescent overhead lighting.

Arlington Fawole is *stoic*, and the people around him, friends and coworkers, would describe him as such. So they say.

Arlington Fawole is tall, a few inches over six feet. Because of this, and because of his regal Nigerian posture, he appears to be much stronger and more formidable than he actually is. But I know the truth. I know about his sloppy spider's egg sac belly. That bulbous bulge that betrays him. I know he is actually lazy. I know that if I gripped both sides of his stomach fat with my hands and held it out, slightly extending it, I could flop it up and down like a thermal blanket, or a rubber blanket, like the type they use in detox rooms for junkies. Disgusting.

Arlington Fawole is disgusting, and what makes him disgusting is not that he is fat. What makes him disgusting is that he keeps the people around him fooled. Fooled into thinking he is stoic and strong, a masterclass in discipline and moderation. But in reality, he is no different than the rest of us.

"Well," I say, leaning in and snatching the file off his desk. "I never said any of this."

He reaches for the file. His fingers graze an edge. "You can't!"

I look over the file, act like I'm reading what's inside. I put it back on the desk with his *Best Dad Ever* mug and his framed pictures of his stupid family and the rest of his stupid life. "Like I said, I never said any of this."

"You can't just say you didn't say something," he whines. "It's a signed statement. And there were witnesses."

"Listen," I say, standing up and heading for the door. When I reach it, I turn back around and stare daggers into Arlington.

It's giving Stygian void eyes.

It's giving instant cell death.

"None of this happened. This whole thing is stupid. I'm saving lives and you come at me with this shit?"

Arlington Fawole looks positively flabbergasted.

I imagine him telling his friends that he would never live in Baltimore, and that Crofton provides the far superior Anne Arundel County school system and is still a reasonable distance to Hopkins as far as commutes go.

I imagine Arlington Fawole's shiny brown pate splitting open. The way I see it, a dark, red line stretches from the space between his eyes, backwards up his forehead, bisecting his sweaty scalp. The skin peels back, no, *shrinks* back, receding down the sides of his face, folds of puffy flesh crumpling up at his ears like a foreskin. Inside of his skull, much is revealed. It is a bright golden light. It shines through. This golden light is made of Arlington's lies, his amplified mask.

"You're a child passenger safety technician," he exhales.

I fake incredulous. "And now you condescend to me? You demean me? Make light of my work?"

"I didn't mean it like—"

"Don't do that," I say. From the door where I stand it's like I'm hovering over him, colossal. For this moment, my insides feel warm and good. Full. Like pound cake. "Don't fall back now. Stand on what you said. I'm just a child passenger safety technician. What I do isn't important. I get it. That's what I'll be telling *your* superior."

I take an absurdly long amount of time closing the door to his office when I leave and the whole time I'm doing it, he's telling me that I don't need to close the door, that it's OK, that I can leave it open, and the door is making this slow creaking sound, and his voice starts tearing open my uterus and the tearing doesn't stop until I close the door and I can no longer hear his mouth diarrhea.

CHAPTER 6

PERCOCET HELPS, BUT NOT AS MUCH AS OXY OR heroin, and that's because you can't take enough of it. This is on account of the Tylenol. It fucks with your liver, makes your lower back hurt. Take too many Percs and you feel like Gervonta Davis used your kidneys as training bags.

The maximum dose of acetaminophen an adult can ingest safely within a 4-6 hour period is about 1000mg. A single $10 Perc sold in front of Lexington Market has only 5mg of oxycodone hydrochloride and a whopping 325mg of acetaminophen. This means that three Percs is the max you can take before you cause yourself more pain than whatever pain you're trying to numb with the Percs in the first place, and three pills ain't shit. Certainly not enough opiates to do anything beyond make you frustrated and wish you had more.

There is something you *can* do however. There is always a solution, always a way out. This solution has an air of mystique to it. The formula is treated like an esoteric text, like forbidden knowledge. Like the Necronomicon, or the Tabula Smaragdina, but for drugs. So many people don't even know it exists. Until now.

This is what you do:

Crush ten pills into a fine powder, then stir thoroughly in a glass of warm water. Put the glass in the freezer and let sit for twenty minutes. At this point, the mixture will have separated. Take the glass out of the freezer and get another glass of the same size. Place a coffee filter on the mouth of the new glass. Pour the liquid slowly into the new glass through the coffee filter. If done correctly, after passing through the coffee filter, the liquid should now have a gray color, like industrial waste water. See that muddy white residue caught in the coffee filter? That's the acetaminophen. That's what you don't want. Throw that shit away. Repeat the process one, maybe two more times. Now drink that glass of gray liquid. It tastes like shit. That's your pure oxycodone.

I typically keep my mix in a Stanley Quencher H2.0, stainless steel, vacuum insulated tumbler. It's from Stanley's *Soft Matte* collection. I went with *Stormy Sea,* which is a dark, teal color. I like how the rubberized finish feels on my skin.

I unlock my phone and stare at the screen. Instagram, Twitter, Facebook, TikTok—all lit up with red notification bubbles. I check Instagram first. When I click the *home* button, it takes me to my feed. Across the top of the screen are profile bubbles of people who have uploaded recent stories. The first one is MrSouthwest, a guy named Korey DeJesus who tried to make me give him head in the stairwell at Mervo when he was a senior and I was a sopho-more. I click on his story.

The video is Korey in the passenger seat of his friends convertible, singing along to *Fuck Up Some Commas*. His friend sings along too, one hand on the wheel, the other throwing up gang signs of neigh-borhoods neither of them have ever lived in.

It's giving lame.

It's giving fuck boy.

The story flips over to a video of Korey and his friend at a pool party, a new song, this one I don't recognize, playing in the background. The story flips again and it's a still image of a doberman with gold teeth. The owner is peeling the dog's lips back with his or her index and thumb to show the shiny teeth.

The story flips over to Amber's latest story. If you let it ride, the story feature on Instagram will just keep showing you the next person's stories, and then the next person after that, and so on. So here we are, arriving at the window to Amber's life. She's at the Waldorf Astoria again. This time, the one in Vegas. I know this, because her first Instagram story is a still image of the menu from the Waldorf Astoria, and below the words *Waldorf Astoria*, are two smaller words, which say *Las* and *Vegas*.

It's giving bad bitch.

It's giving boss bitch.

The next story Amber shares is a Boomer-ang clip of her hand and the hands of four other women—you can tell by the pastel stiletto nails, the

jewelry, the hand and wrist tattoos of hearts and semicolons—holding champagne flutes and clinking them together. The action goes in reverse and then repeats itself in the correct direction, then goes in reverse, and repeats itself correctly again, and continues doing this until the Boomerang clip is gone and replaced with a new story.

CHAPTER 7

Amiri Shirt is still sitting on my serpentine sofa in the same position I left him in and he's starting to get ripe.

I make something to eat—Velveeta 3-½ minute mac and cheese and an orange soda because I love orange things—then sit down next to Amiri Shirt and check out the latest episode of my favorite dating and relationship reality television series, *The Whale*.

The Whale is a reality-TV dating show where an unidentified individual known only as the Whale is provided with a pool of sixteen women who are all vying for his affection and, potentially, a long-term relationship or marriage. The show follows a structured format where the Whale goes on a series of dates with the contestants, ranging from group dates to one-on-one experiences. However, unlike many other relationship reality television shows oversaturating the market, in *The Whale*, the Whale is never revealed. We are never shown the Whale's face, body, nothing. We assume that the Whale is positioned somewhere behind a mobile, thirty-foot-tall, burgundy velvet curtain, and we can assume this because the women are instructed to speak to the curtain, which is always present when they go on dates or compete in various challenges for the Whale's affection.

We can assume that someone, or something, is behind the curtain, because a voice can be heard speaking through it, and there are a plethora of wires running behind the curtain that we can assume must connect to microphones for amplifying the Whale's voice. However, the voice we hear is robotic, like an archaic voice box provided to someone post-laryngeal surgery, and because of this, we can not assume that it is actually the Whale behind the curtain, but because we have no reference for what the Whale looks like, sounds like, or even is, we must assume that it is the Whale behind the curtain for the sake of enjoying the show.

Throughout the episodes, contestants are eliminated during ceremonies called "Ambergris Brunches" where the Whale—or what we must assume is the Whale behind the curtain—spits out, or vomits up a massive boulder of neon orange material which launches over the top of the curtain rod and lands on the contestant being eliminated, killing them instantly.

At this point, we hear the voice box-from-behind-the-curtain-that-we-must-assume-is-the-Whale scream, "I'm the Whale! I'm the Whale!"

We know that the Whale is screaming because his words distort the robotic voice.

I finish my mac and cheese and after this week's episode of the Whale—this time an Eritrean data analyst from Philadelphia was eliminated, her body crumpling like an accordion under the mass of ambergris—and because Amiri Shirt is starting to smell worse, and because of the fact that I don't feel like moving him, I go out for a jog.

I suckle at the cold night like a piglet, drink it down like it will soothe whatever madness is going on inside of me. I exhale, watch my breath turn into vapor clouds. My feet start hitting the ground, I'm picking up speed and the cold air coming in from the Bay feels good against my skin. My muscles start to warm up. I get a good rhythm going with my breathing and pace.

I make a left on Golden Ring and pass Dimmples Car Rentals on my right. I maintain a steady cadence, hitting the ground first with the ball of my foot, then rolling to the heel before pushing off again.

My breathing syncs up with the tempo of my footfalls. I drop off the sidewalk at Kern Ave and start running in the street. I zip and I zag until I'm running in the direction of oncoming traffic. I keep going towards Philadelphia Ave when a white Acura Legend with 5% tints comes barreling at me. I don't stop. I don't get out of its way. I just keep running at the Acura until it swerves into the Rosedale Federal Savings and Loan Association in an attempt to avoid hitting me, flipping onto its nose and pole-vaulting over a fire hydrant, landing on its roof with a sickening crunch.

It does nothing for my pelvic cramps so I run around the Walgreens twice and then stop to catch my breath in the parking lot. I dry swallow two

Klonopins and watch a video on my phone of the Gaza Strip after an IDF airstrike in the border city of Rafah. In the clip, a man holds a limp child in his arms and screams in Arabic. The child is no more than four or five and the man holding the child appears to be fairly young himself, mid-twenties or so. The force of the man's screaming shakes the child and the child's head flops back like a puppet, hanging unnaturally. The eyes are clicked back like a doll's, glassy, seeing nothing. The child's face is gray, like it's made of volcanic ash, like a stale sugar cookie. Like if the man keeps shaking the child, its head will come apart like the ash end of a cigarette.

The pair are surrounded by others. Red and white checkered keffiyehs abound. The skin of the man's face pulls tight with each bellowed word, his eyes leaking tears.

I suck my tongue with my lips held together until I can produce enough spit to pop another Klonopin. It's not quite enough saliva, so I taste too much of the pill going down. It's bitter. It bites the center of my tongue and sinks deep into it like a stain.

I jog back to where the flipped Acura is for a closer look. Most of the lights in the parking lot of the Rosedale Federal Savings and Loan Association have gone bad, bathing the wreckage in a purple glow. The white Acura looks robin egg blue under the lighting. Smoke leaks from the front of the car. Twisted metal, scattered debris. Burnt rubber and oil clogging up the air, turning the taste of breath acrid.

The upturned body exposes the intricate network of mechanical parts that make up the underbelly of the vehicle. It looks like twisting reproductive organs. I almost vomit. More lazy tendrils of smoke drift upwards from where the gas tank is.

The windshield and driver side window are spiderwebbed into a mosaic of shattered glass. Through the chaotic mosaic, I can see the muddy shape of a person. The airbags—having exploded into protective balloons—obfuscate the face of the driver. I cannot tell if they are alive or dead.

I get closer. Broken glass crunches under my sneakers. The person behind the exploded steering wheel moves.

I say, "Hey, hey. Wait. You probably shouldn't move."

They shake, jerk back. Shake again, white knuckled. Try to pull back. They manage to pull away from the pillow far enough to get their head turned to the side so that they're looking at me with one bloody eye. A young man. He tries to speak and blood runs over his bottom lip, pooling in a shallow depression in the exploded airbag.

"What?" I ask.

"Hemph."

"Hemph?" I giggle. "What is *hemph* supposed to mean?"

"Hemph," he says. "Peas hemph. Peas? Hemph peas."

Now he's got me cackling. "Peas and hemp? What the fuck?"

"Help!" He spits up more blood then falls into a coughing fit.

"Oh, I get it!" I say. "I get it now. You were saying 'please help' not 'peas and hemp.' That makes so much more sense now. Fuck, man."

The man makes noises from the bottom of his throat that sound like the last thirty seconds of a Keurig coffee machine as it finishes dispensing a cup.

I get close enough to feel the fever radiating off of his body. "When my father died, we had to go through all of his belongings, figure out what to keep and what to get rid of," I tell him. "We found a box filled with portraits, charcoal sketches of faces. Most of the faces looked Arab, some kind of Middle Eastern people. They were pretty good, actually."

The man makes deepthroat gagging noises.

"Anyway, we find out later from my grandmother that after he got back from Kuwait, he started this thing where he would draw the faces of the men he killed. Told her that it helped him let them go, that it was the only way he could lose their ghosts. It's amazing what people will do for their ghosts, you know what I mean?"

He dies and I smell shit.

This makes me feel better. I'm not the reason he's dead, but I'm not the reason he's not not dead either.

Everything stinks. Now he stinks, the air stinks, and I have to go back home to stinking Amiri Shirt.

CHAPTER 8

On my serpentine sofa, where you can tell I'm thick as fuck even when I'm sitting down because of the way my thighs and cheeks spread out, inhaling the rotten pineapple dumpster juice stink of Amiri Shirt, tapping the Facebook icon on my phone screen to open up the app, and from there, I tap my profile image which takes me to a bunch of tab options. This is how I get to my Facebook Groups. My favorite group out of all the groups I belong to is Nursing Connections.

According to their *about section*, Nursing Connections is a platform where you can seek out or offer support, encouragement, advice and share stories and best practices. This group is to motivate you to be the best nurse you can be. Feel free to share updates about healthcare, study sheets for continuing education, resume help, networking, etc. Our mission in this group is to empower you and other nurses and nursing students through the community.

That's what it says in their *about* section.

It also says: Nurses are the <3 of healthcare!!!

There are exactly three exclamation points after the word *healthcare* and this is to let you know that nurses *really* are the heart of healthcare, and if you do not recognize this, a pack of nurses will create a TikTok where they do a choreographed dance routine with captions talking about what a shitty patient you are. This will go viral. The music in the background will be Beyoncé - "Break My Soul" and the dancing ability of the nurses will be decent, and you will watch it, and you will wonder how they had time to come up with the routine, commit it to memory, and record the video.

I'm pretty popular in the group. I like to post memes of patients being annoying. An image of a demonic creature rapping on the glass and staring at the viewer of the image with a caption above that reads: Patients when it's 7:55am. A bright, white block letter caption that says: MFW a patient doesn't control their kid in the waiting area and then below the caption is an image of Casey Anthony looking exasperated. A lot of people like my memes and laugh react to them. They leave comments too, encouraging things like: *she's back!* and *GIRL YOU ARE CRAZY.*

I make my own memes and the people in Nursing Connections know this. I use an app called Mematic for the template generators and when I'm working on something more intricate, I also use Pic-Stitch to create the layouts I want.

Occasionally, somebody will leave a disparaging comment that says something like: *How does she have time to make these?* and this fills me with a sick, muddy purple hate, and it's purple and muddy because I'm sad now too. I think about how I want to hurt them like they hurt me. I think about how I want to eat their faces and then take Miralax so that I shit out the liquid version of their faces while they're screaming with their face-skin gone, or while they're passed out from screaming and bleeding for so long, and then I want to smack them in their skinless faces until they gain conscious and then make them drink their liquid face diarrhea.

And then, I scroll down a bit and see that someone else has left a comment that says: *hey, come on, give her a break,* and then I feel better and I almost feel good. Then I take a deep breath and go back to scrolling the group feed where I will see a post from Shatara Wellborne that says: *I wish Medicaid woulda mailed all the patients a letter explaining the changes on what's no longer covered and the deductions on allowance amounts* and an exasperated-groaning emoji for emphasis. The first comment will say: *even if they did, the pt wouldn't read it!* And then two laughing-until-crying emojis. The comment after that will say: *she's right, people wouldn't read it anyway, so providers have to explain it all. I am so tired of patients saying Medicaid covers everything. No sir, they do not!*

With my confidence restored, I will leave a funny comment that says: *y'all patients can read?* and embedded in the comment will be the GIF from the movie *We're the Millers* where Will Poulet's character

finds out that he is the only one not getting paid for their drug smuggling excursion. I will laugh to myself at my cleverness and wait as the likes and loves and laugh reactions stack up and ding ding ding on my phone and vibrate me.

And then I cum.

The first post that pops up in the main feed for Nursing Connections is from Kimeya Daniels. Kimeya is from Lake Jackson, Florida and works for UTMB, which is a lively 24-hour urgent care clinic in the ghetto, in a dated strip mall sandwiched between a Dollar Tree and a Suboxone doc box.

Kimeya's post says: had a patient say "oh you're here for me" and touched my lower lowerrrrrrrrr back, his hand was on the top of my (PEACH EMOJI), and pull me closer to him while escorting him from triage to the exam room. When i reported it to my boss, she brushes it off and say "oh hes just one of those really nice older guys, hes been coming here for years."

How's everyone else's day going? Thank goodness my last day is Friday.

(FACEPALM BLONDE WOMAN EMOJI)

I tap the COMMENT tab below the post to expand the window and see what everyone is saying.

The first comment is from Laken Reed of Lawton, Oklahoma: I had a patient tell me he liked the way my fingers stroked the keyboard (VOMITING EMOJI)

Leana Martin of Durango, Colorado replies to Laken Reed's comment with: Ewwwwwwww. I would never allow my staff to be treated that way.

I tap the comment bubble and start typing and lying: I once had a patient who was obsessed with my feet! WTF! Like, he would call to see if I was working and then bring me donuts. I threw the donuts out every time, he was so creepy!
(GREEN SICK FACE EMOJI)

I'm kind of a big deal in Nursing Connections.

Before I can press the navy blue paper plane icon in the lower right-hand corner that posts my comment, my screen goes black and tells me I have an incoming call from UNKNOWN.

I press the green circle that says ANSWER, then press the gray circle that changes the audio to speaker. "Hello?"

There's a faint buzzing on the line. Like a power drill, but muffled. Then chitinous clicking.

"Hello?"

The buzzing and clicking become louder, clearer, more defined. It sounds less like mechanical buzzing. More like a cricket, or a katydid, and then it's louder and louder and it's almost like a person saying, "dinga dinga dinga dinga dinga," through a poor connection, through a distorted microphone from far away.

"Fuck you then!" I scream into the phone, and when I scream, little bits of spittle fly out of my mouth and when the spit globules land on the screen they look like iridescent glass beads.

I press the red circle to end the call.

CHAPTER 9

On the way to work the next morning, I listen to a recap podcast about *The Whale*.

The name of the show is *Whale Watching*, hosted by 031 Bleeder and Tokyo Tiffany. I typically like to listen the morning after watching the latest episode, so I can stay up to date with the latest news about the contestants. See, the thing about reality dating shows is that they are recorded way in advance, so what you are watching on TV is old news. The contestant who hasn't won yet on the show, but already has in real life, might not even be currently dating the Whale. Perhaps they have broken up by now, seeing as how whatever outcome occurred in the recording of the season finale is something that has already come and gone.

On *Whale Watching*, Bleeder and Tiffany recap the most recent episode of *The Whale*, but they also keep you up to date with what's going on with the contestants in real time. A lot of the girls end up becoming celebrities in their own right. If they made a big enough impression on the fans during their time

 55 

on the show before being eliminated, and they manage to survive the Ambergris Brunch, well, they usually end up getting a show of their own.

I drive slow in the furthest right lane of the Pulaski Highway so I can catch all eighteen minutes of the show before I get to the parking garage at Hopkins where I lose reception.

The sound of a sine wave comes out of my car speakers. Electrical saw warbling. The sound of glass shattering, then tinkling. "You're here with Tokyo Tiffany," says a woman's voice.

"And 031 Bleeder, bitch!" growls a man's baritone.

"And we're here to get you up to date on what's going on in the Whale's world," the woman says. "Your number one source for everything Whale-related. If they're talking about the Whale, they got it from us." The sound of ice in a glass. The sound of Tiffany sipping something in the mic. "Bleed, baby, did you hear what Sharde is up to?"

"Shit, what she doing?" asks 031 Bleeder.

"OK, first of all, this bitch is crazy. A few days ago, she posted that she was gonna start an OnlyFans."

"An OnlyFans? That's not crazy. Let shordie get her bag. Get that money shordie."

"No, I know that!" says Tokyo Tiffany. "What I'm saying is, she posts that she's gonna start this OnlyFans and the night it goes live, she has one million paid subscribers almost instantly."

"One million?" 031 Bleeder sounds like he's pretending to be surprised.

"One million. Crazy. She's over two now. This bitch is gonna be rich before me."

The sound of ice in a glass. Clinking. More sipping, swallowing.

On my left, buildings whiz by, looming warehouses filled with marble and granite or paint supplies. On my right, vacant buildings without roofs, probably lost in fires. Boarded up windows and shuttered auto part stores and pallet services. An abandoned gas station, everything but the barrel vault roof and concrete pillars gone.

"So, like, how do that shit work, though?" asks Bleeder. "Like, she got an OF but she ain't got no arms or legs? How do she set up the cameras and all that?"

Tokyo Tiffany snorts. "I mean, I assume she has help."

"If y'all been living under a rock or something," says Bleeder, "then y'all might have missed what happened to Sharde in the beginning of the season."

"That's right, people" says Tiffany. "You might remember that Sharde lost her legs *and* her arms when she was eliminated."

"This bitch ain't got no legs!" barks Bleeder. "Or arms!"

He's from Southern California, Pomona to be precise, so he pronounces the word *arms* with an almost comically rhotic R. When I think about rhotic R's, I think about the Irish of Boston. I think about how they have no rhotic R now, how the children of Irish immigrants ended up adopting the already

established local accent of the colonial-era settlers from East Anglia. How they became what they heard around them. How they allowed their rhoticity to be raped from them and replaced with the non-rhotic Received Pronunciation speech of their Puritan enemies. Then I start thinking about all the things people try to take from me. Then I'm thinking about all the things I can take from people and which of those things counts the most.

Something hits the hood of my car and explodes. It's like bird shit spraying everywhere, but it doesn't drip, it hangs and freezes. I see it dangle off my side mirrors as I drive, trying to find somewhere to pull over.

I put my car in park in the shoulder lane and turn my hazards on. The white bird shit-looking stuff has splattered the hood of my car like the toe of a 2022 Timberland Paint Splash boot. Big gobs of the stuff hang off the fender, some of it clumps up in the headlights too. I scrape some of it with my nail but it doesn't come off. Bits of the thicker areas chip off until my thumbnail splits, but it's only the top layer. Where the substance touches the paint of the car, it just *is*. Like it's become part of the car.

I get my ice scraper out of the trunk and try that. I'm pushing, scraping, trying to pry off the layers of thick, opaque material that streaks the front of my car and windshield in long soupy ropes.

Like cum. Endless cum. Completely full of cum.

I stop when I realize that the cum-shit is not the only thing I'm scraping. The ice scraper is brutal, taking off pieces of the paint with it, leaving streaks and scratches on the hood. The windshield is different. I can work with the windshield. I can use the ice scraper on the windshield and it doesn't damage anything. I get most of the bird shit cum off the glass but it leaves slug trails of adhesive. Shiny cellophane sheets.

I have to get to work now so I decide to deal with this later. I get back in the car and lean to the right while driving, almost until my elbow is in the passenger seat, so I can see through the Milky Way galaxy of streaks and striations that cum-stain the windshield.

CHAPTER 10

PPHIL'S IN THE BREAK ROOM, TRYING TO TALK TO me again, asking me if I did anything cool over the weekend. "I don't want anything to be weird between us," he says, not really looking at me. "Things can go back to the way they used to be."

"How's that?" I ask.

"You know, the way things used to."

I don't respond. I make the silence fat. Make him sit with his shit a little longer. I turn my back to him and pop a Klonopin. I stare at my phone screen until my face unlocks it, then check Instagram, Tik-Tok, Facebook, Twitter—in that order.

This bitch I know, Amber, her IG Story consists of pics from the Waldorf Astoria, of the menu at Sushi Nakazawa, the bar at Peacock Alley. And then, a pic of her shoes: Jimmy Choo, of course. A pic of her plate, a pic of her raspberry and passion fruit martini. I have no idea what this bitch does, how she can afford all this. I never see her post a status about work, or anything work related. She never complains or uses her social media to *vent*.

Ever.

Phil still won't look at me. "Do anything cool over the weekend?"

I fucking *adore* Amber. I put my phone back in my scrubs and say, "No, but did you know that in 1997, Cal Ripken walked in on his wife getting her back blown out by none other than Kevin Costner, and the Orioles staged a power outage during their game against the Mariners to keep Cal's record streak alive? Cal couldn't make it to the game, you see, on account of the Costner thing. Some people say he missed the game because he beat the shit out of Kevin Costner and spent the night in jail. Some people say he missed the game because he beat the shit out of his wife and spent the night in jail. Either way, somebody got the shit beat out of them. Honestly, I hope it was both. His wife for being a whore and Kevin Costner for that movie *Dances With Wolves*. What a fucking dumpster fire that was. He really shit the bed with that one. Plus, I love the Orioles. Fuck Kevin Costner."

Phil gapes. Sputters. "People loved *Dancing with Wolves*."

"What people?"

"It won seven Academy Awards!"

"Nobody even dances with any wolves in it. I watched the whole thing, Phil, and not one wolf dances. It's stupid, Phil."

He swipes at his phone furiously. "It has an 87% rating on Rotten Tomatoes!"

"Fuck you, Phil!" I shout, pointing at him, my finger so close to his eyeball that I can feel the wetness vibrating off his sclera. "You're a stupid fucking bitch, Phil. That's what you are. You like *Dances with Wolves* and Kevin Costner and Cal Ripken's whore wife and asking people what they did over the weekend so you can talk about what you did over *your* weekend. Well I'm not gonna let you have that, Phil. You hear me? You will never tell me what you did over the weekend. Never!"

Phil looks at me like I just stuck my finger in his asshole. This observation is redundant because Phil's mouth already looks like an asshole. "Is everything good with you, Jada?" he asks.

And then I'm fixating on Phil's sphincter-mouth. His wormy chitterling lips. How the wrinkles tattoo the corners of his mouth like pink henna, the long lines that starfish his philtrum like the raw skin of a fucked asshole. How his lips are like his mouth-anus prolapsed. How if I put my fist inside his mouth he would look just like a blown out colon. How his dysgenic cartilage chin sinks into his neck. His jowls. His scaly eczema scalp, like one of the babies with cradle cap. His stupid red bell pepper nose.

It feels like *my* nose just started bleeding. "I'm fine, Phil!"

I storm out of the break room, but not before doubling over and clutching my gut and spitting out a clot of blood that hits the floor with a smack like a wet sock.

"Are you sure you're good?" Phil asks as I regain my composure.

I choke down copper and iron and give one last, "Fuck you, Phil!" at the top of my lungs before throwing myself out the door.

CHAPTER 11

I REACH OUT TO TWO DIFFERENT LUXURY DETAIL companies via email. One of them responds to my email while I'm with a patient, asking me to send them pictures of the damage, so when I'm finished reviewing child passenger car seat safety with the new mother and her boyfriend or husband, I go out to the parking lot where my car is and circle around the front of it, flicking pictures.

The streaks of bird cum shit look like a topographical map of Crazy Peak, Montana, but eggshell-white now after drying in the sun. I snap more pictures and attach them to my reply emails. Hit send.

The company's name is Woodlawn Mobile Car Clinic and they tell me that they can take care of the damage, that it will run me $300 because they'll have to use a special compound to remove whatever the bird shit cum is. They're a mobile detailer, so they explain that they'll come to me, which is another separate fee, even though *me* going to *them* is not an option they offer. I give them the address to the garage in front of Hopkins. They tell me that they'll call when they're out front, and that I can take the keys downstairs to them. That it will take a few hours, and they'll call again when they're finished.

Back at the hospital, I move my body and mind like an automaton. In the patient's room. The new mother's room. I'm checking the car seat in the room, looking it up in my car seat bible, inspecting all the buttons and straps. I check the infant's outfit. Is it safe? Will there be snagging?

The mobile detailer calls and I miss it. I run down the stairs and out of the hospital and across the street to the garage where I see him in the back where my car is parked against the wall.

"Hey, how's it going?" he says. He's stocky, dark skinned and he looks at me like he's hungry, like he wants to stuff me with things.

I smile, shake my head. "What do you think it is?" I hand him my keys.

He runs his thumb against an off-white streak of chunks on the hood of my car. Scrapes it a bit with his nail. "Expansion foam, maybe?"

He says it like a question, like he doesn't really know either.

"Yeah, I can see that."

He scrapes a bit more with his thumb and then stands back. "What you say happened?"

I frown. "I didn't."

"Well, if I knew what it was, I could probably do a better job helping you out. I'd know what to use to get it off."

"I was driving, listening to this podcast and—"

"Podcast?" He cuts me off. "I love podcasts. I'm actually thinking about starting my own podcast, about mobile detailing."

I feel like my stomach is full of hydrochloric acid. I feel like my pussy is being choked with lengths of barbed tubing. I feel like the tubes are wrapping around my calves and snaking up my thighs and into my slit, like the tubes are going inside of me and pushing up until they tap the cervix, and the barbs get caught on my walls when the tubes try to retract, pulling out ropes of me, the black skeins of my insides.

"I have to get back to work," I tell him, turning and heading back to the hospital.

"Sure," he says. "I'll text you soon as I'm done. I'll tell you about my idea for the podcast later. I can really see you being involved in some kind of way."

Back upstairs in Labor and Delivery, I can't allow mother and child to leave the wing until I ensure the child will be safe in the car seat; that I can fit two fingers under the restraints with the child in it, that I've made sure that the baby's clothes are not too thick, but also not too thin, and that I can put the baby in the car seat. I must inspect form and function, then go to the car itself to confirm the seat is not too big to fit in it safely. This must be done. I must confirm that the boyfriend or husband can put the seat in, to make sure he can do it correctly, safely, so next, the CPST, which is me, disables the GPS tracking device on the infant's umbilical cord and takes the baby in the car seat to meet the boyfriend or husband at the car, to put the seat in with the boyfriend or husband.

My phone vibrates my hip bone and electricity warps my orbital bone structure. It's the mobile detailer with the podcast. The message says: ALL GOOD with a thumbs up emoji.

I finish with my patient, run down the stairs, back to the garage. The bird shit cum is still all over the car. Nothing has changed. It's like he did nothing. Like he was never there.

"Yeah," he says, wistful expression on his smooth face. "I don't know what to tell you. It's gotta be something like expansion foam. Some kind of epoxy."

"So you couldn't do anything?"

He looks nonplussed. Like I've offended his mobile detailing sensibilities. "Anything? Of course I did. Look at your car, babygirl. Just look at it. Luxury detailing a car involves meticulous work. I hand washed it. Waxed it. Hit it with the ceramic coating, interior vacuuming, steam cleaning, leather conditioning, all that there, babygirl."

If he calls me babygirl again I'm going to release my second set of pharyngeal jaws and bite off his chin. Like a moray eel. I'm going to chew and chew until masticated bits of face meat fall from my lips and dribble down my chin like muffin crumbs. "But you couldn't get any of the cum shit off? So you detailed the rest of the car and just left the cum on? I didn't even need all that, man, I just wanted you to get the bird shit cum off."

"Say what now?" He shifts from foot to foot.

We look at the car together.

"This isn't fair."

"You can give me half," he says with a sheepish grin. "I can do Venmo. CashApp cool too. Or just cash."

I Venmo him $150 which means I'm going to have to figure out another way to pay the BGE bill this month. He thanks me and flashes more fluorescent teeth. I still need to figure out what to do about the bird shit cum.

CHAPTER 12

Back at my apartment, Amiri Shirt from the other night at Euphoria decomposes in my bathtub. I use the machete to make a cut into his thigh, two more into his calf in the shape of a cross. After removing the fat and muscle and facial features, I break him down with a cat's paw and a liberal amount of pressure, prying him apart at the joints. I use channel-lock pliers to twist the cartilage until the ligaments pop.

I do this because of this shit called ASMR that stupid people are into. It actually is real though.

I'm using various tools and kitchen appliances—chopping and cutting and separating and grating. I press down on unfamiliar masses with my hands, pummel them with my fists. I pull apart strings of meat and flesh with my fingers, some of it with my teeth.

Expansion foam? How the fuck?

I neglect to wash my hands before I pick up my phone and start swiping. I'm too anxious, too full of energy, too full of love. My insides are warm and I

don't want to mess up the vibe so I'm swiping until I find the Janelle Monae song I'm looking for and let it ride. That warm, oceanic, slow build of organs and guitars and gasping backing vocals kicks in.

The hi-hats roll out and I use a lemon zester on his right ass cheek, running it back and forth, turning his flesh into thin ribbons of skin, twirling up and around like mauve curly fries. I draw the zester across his peel, separating zest from pith.

I sing along with Janelle, "Told the whole world, I'm the venom and the antidote, takes a different type of girl to keep the whole world afloat!"

I pinch pieces of zest between my fingers and nibble ends. I flick the ribbons, watch them flutter. I'm covered in pieces of Amiri Shirt but like Janelle says, *I don't care what I look like because I feel good, better than amazing, and better than I could.*

God I feel good.

When it comes to his separated parts, I stuff what I can down the shower drain, and what is too big to fit, I flush down the toilet or feed to the garbage disposal. By the time I feel like I'm done, he's greatly reduced. Just a pile of miscellaneous parts in my bathtub, the useless accouterments of what used to be a body.

I check Instagram, TikTok, Facebook, Twitter—in that order.

I check Amber's IG Story. The first pic is one of those inspirational quotes in Courier New on top of a background image of flowers, blurred out of focus so that you can read the white text on top of it. It says, "The absence of someone, God can fill. But the absence of God, no one can fill."

The motivational quote image disappears and is replaced by a new one: a solid black square with a line of white text in Courier New. It says, "I want to be on an island with my ass out eating fruit and margaritas rn."

"Whole Lotta Money" by BIA plays in the background. All of her stories, her reels, every single one is giving bad bitch. I fucking *adore* Amber. I put my phone down on the Formica countertop and go to the bathroom.

I work every day this week, and since the tub is currently occupied, I take a hoe bath in the sink, splashing cold water on my face and under my armpits. I shrug into my navy blue scrubs and throw my locs in a loose bun. I get in my car, hit the push-to-start and just sit there, thinking about all the people I haven't done anything to yet. I start thinking about how many people there are and it's hard for me to breathe. I read in *National Geographic Kids* that there are as many habitable planets in our universe as there are grains of sand on earth, and I remember when I read it I felt physically ill, nauseous, wondering how anyone could possibly count grains of sand, let alone all the sand on earth? It would be impossible. So the quantity of habitable planets was a lie, and would always be a lie.

I'm having trouble breathing, like I can't take a full breath, like there's a belt around my lungs refusing to allow them to expand. I take two Klonopins with water from the kitchen faucet. There are some quantities that are just too big for us to manage.

CHAPTER 13

When your baby dies in childbirth, the NICU nurses give you single-line exhaustible dialogue responses in relation to the type of hospital they work for. At Holy Cross, in Silver Spring, the NICU nurses will ask the mother if they want to spend more time with the dying or recently deceased baby. They will ask you if you want to take a picture with the baby, or baby corpse, even offer to take the pictures so you and your partner, if you have one, don't have to hold the phone and the dead baby at the same time and take the picture in that selfie way people do. They will tell the recently baby-less mother that the baby is in a better place.

This is because Holy Cross is a Catholic hospital. This is part of their branding, their mission statement.

At Hopkins, where I work, we're much more sensible. Prudent. Practical. We give the mother some pamphlets, some resources where they can meet other women like themselves, women who have seen the light at the end of the tunnel and made it to the other side. Potential protectors, sponsors, big sisters.

And our equipment is better too. State of the art. We have this machine the urologists use called the Da Vinci II. It's remote surgery through robotics and augmented reality. If you get shot in your dick or pussy, you definitely want to get airlifted to Hopkins, if you want any chance of surviving, that is. I read a study that showed how Baltimore's murder rate would be higher if it wasn't for Hopkins's world-renowned trauma unit.

I am a child passenger safety technician.

What this means is that I paid $95 and went to the four-day CPS certification course. It's through an organization called Safe Kids. I passed the written tests and hands-on skills assessment. They gave me a CPST card to keep in my wallet or laminate and hang around my neck on a Ravens (I assume) lanyard. The most difficult part was getting the $95 together and not spending it on something else the moment I had it.

I had to recite this child passenger safety technician creed, like the pledge of allegiance, or the serenity prayer. It was something about how as a CPS technician I solemnly swear to provide unbiased information with the goal of helping caregivers select a car seat, making certain that my recommendations are based on the specific needs of the family, and to not make recommendations based solely on brand and/or personal preference.

But I can, though, if I want to. I can tell the new mother that the best car seat—if she cares *at all* about

the safety of her child—is the Graco Tranzitions 3-in-1. I'm not saying it is, I'm saying I could tell her that. Get endless sales for Graco if I wanted to. I don't want to, but it's the *knowing* that I have this power that's one of the few perks of this job for me.

I am the lord of that realm, the god of that universe. The universe where I decide if you get to leave with your baby.

That little name tag device attached to your baby's umbilical cord? That piece of plastic has a device in it that alerts the hospital's security system if you try to leave with your baby before finishing the Child Passenger Safety class. It makes all the magnetic doors in the birthing center auto-lock, so that you can't escape with your baby, so you can't make it downstairs to the first level where the parking garage is.

I decide whether you take your little bundle of joy home.

I have to complete a series of screens, check the right boxes, sign it with my digital signature at the end. This lets the head nurse on duty know you're good to go. And it's just me that holds this unimaginable power. There's also the charge nurse who comes in and reminds you not to shake your baby. The SIDS speech, they call it. Usually they bring us in at the same time: me to help you not kill your baby with a vehicle, her to help you not kill your baby with frustration.

"Now listen," she says. "You no shake your baby."

The new parents nod.

"No seriously, don't shake her."

The new parents look at each other.

"Serious, honey," she likes to say. "Don't do it. Your baby's head is stupid-big compared to the rest of her body. If you don't give it support, her head is gonna flop around because the neck muscles ain't strong enough to hold it still. When you shake your baby, you're throwing her big-old head back and forth, fast and with great force, and this force causes tiny blood vessels inside your baby's brain to tear and bleed, resulting in brain damage, or death."

The charge nurse's name is Xiomara and she really makes a show of the whole Don't Shake Your Baby speech. It's like she knows she's ruining a moment for the new parents. Like they're only going to remember *this* moment, this woman telling them not to kill their brand new baby that they could never imagine hurting. Instead of looking at their sleeping precious, yet to open her eyelids, they're thinking about the learning difficulties and disabilities their baby girl is going to have due to them accidentally shaking her when they hug her too hard. Instead of thinking about playing with Legos and all the nights that will be spent reading *Goodnight Moon*, the child's head on their chests, the smell of her scalp; instead they will be wondering what their baby could possibly do to make them shake them.

"Mira, mira," she says. "The type of injuries caused by shaking don't happen by accident. I'm saying, you can't give your little girl shaken baby syndrome by playing with her normally. So you shouldn't stop cuddling with her, playing, doing all the things that you would normally do. The only way to give your baby shaken baby syndrome is by straight up shaking your baby. If it happens, it's *your* fault. That's why you no shake your baby, you understand? Yes? Your actions are the only thing that can kill or brain damage your baby this way. It's totally your fault if it happens. Not up for debate."

When she says the Not Up For Debate part she taps the toe of her Croc on the ground impatiently and I try to muffle a giggle with the back of my hand. It's hard not to laugh when she does this. She's got this serious look on her face, Dominican-abuela serious, and she's tapping her foot to let you know she's not messing around, but her Crocs are neon pink and covered with bling ornaments and shiny accessories. It's the juxtaposition of the ridiculous slides and the serious expression; the foot tapping and the cubic zirconia encrusted BOSS BITCH on the toe of the Croc that's doing the tapping.

Tap tap tap.

It's so hard not to laugh. Meanwhile, the new parents are lightheaded from all this new information.

How does one become that frustrated? he wonders. *Could I ever become that frustrated?* she thinks.

They'll look back on this moment, this supposed-to-be special moment, and all they will remember is this. This memory of death at a time of new life. Of violence towards something you love. Of hurting something you are supposed to protect.

I think Xiomara knows this, knows what she's doing to these people, and I love her for that. "Your

baby is gonna cry, and she gonna cry for plenty of different reasons," she will continue. "Maybe she uncomfortable, maybe she hungry. Maybe she upset or scared. That don't mean you shake her! Goodness. Still, you no shake your baby. Seriously. Just don't do it guys."

Tap tap tap.

"If you feed your baby, you make sure your baby warm, and you love your baby, and your baby still cry, then you did all you can. Nothing more for you to do. This is when you take time for you. Step away from your baby for ten minutes. Maybe you watch TV. Have a quick shower. Or you call a friend, you tell them about your baby making you so frustrated. Still, you *no* shake your baby. Shaking the baby, this not part of deal."

Tap tap tap.

I love that! I love her! I want her to smother me between her enormous Dominican tits and tell me nothing is going to be OK, that nothing will ever get better. I want her to tell me that everything is my fault.

CHAPTER 14

Daneen says that as long as we don't kill anybody on purpose, we've got our jobs for life.

"And even if we did, it'd probably be alright," I say. Laugh a little.

"That's not funny, Jada," and when Daneen says my name, she says it like *Jaduhhhhh* and it's amazing how ugly she can be when she wants to. Waste of meat. Skin puppet. Marionette bones draped in plastic curtains. "Anyway, you're up."

Daneen wheels her cart down the hall and I wheel my contraption—half of the backseat of a car mounted to a dolly—in the other direction. I push my cart in the room, banging it against the door instead of knocking lightly first like I'm supposed to, and the new mother and her baby look like they're made of clay. Or bitumen. Formless. Smooth faces. Formed of clay and bitumen. Nothing but dried up husks. Completely devoid of cum. Empty of all life.

"Hey," the new mother says, flashing a weak smile.

I explain the importance of rear-facing car seats. I emphasize how necessary it is that the car seat is correctly installed. I ask her if she has the car seat she intends on using.

"Yes," she says.

"Is the car seat in the room with us right now?" I question her.

"Huh? Yeah, what? It's right next to you. You're standing right next to it."

I show her how to adjust the harness straps. I show her where the chest clips go. I caution her against using expired or secondhand car seats. I'm encouraging her to do regular inspections when she asks me if I get paid well for doing this. When she asks me this, her words are laced with poison, like she already knows the answer, which she does. I don't know what to say so I tell her the truth.

"Not much, but too much for state insurance," I tell her.

"That's crazy," she says, which is a thing people say when they do not see you as having any value.

I want her to express empathy. I want her to look at me and tell me that I provide an important service and that I help people, but her face is made of clay so I don't see it. Her face is made of bitumen so I don't see her. Her faceless face and her faceless baby.

The new mother takes out her phone and swipes at the screen. She watches the screen, her eyes getting wider and wider.

The audio that comes out of her phone is a man's voice: *tell that fuck boy, wanna play with gang, got the*

*blippy with the beam on it, choppa got the dick with the
titties on it, see that extendo—*

—and then the unmistakable sound of a gunshot.

The new mother shakes her head and holds the
phone out to me. "Have you seen this?" she asks.

I take the phone from her to see what she's talking
about. The screen shows a paused TikTok of a blurry
black man. When I unpause the clip, I see that the
man is young, probably just a teenager. He has shoulder length wicks that stick out, almost horizontally,
because of the thickness of them. He waves a gun with
a comically long clip hanging out of the butt of it. The
green light from the laser attachment below the barrel
periodically flashes the camera lens, turning the Tik-
Tok green, like there's a filter on the video.

The way he looks, the way he talks, I think he's
from Miami, probably Haitian.

The kid waves the gun at the camera, but he's
pointing it at his head. He holds the weapon so
loosely, his trigger discipline atrocious.

He says: *tell that fuck boy, wanna play with gang—*

—I hear a clicking sound that I did not hear
the first time, which appears to be the sound of the
safety being taken off as the kid's precarious fingers
accidentally nudge it.

—*got the blippy with the beam on it, choppa got the
dick with the titties on it, see that extendo—*

—and then the gun goes off, but it is pointed at
his head.

I don't get to see anything because the footage
ends as the phone falls and lands facedown on what

looks like beige carpet. The video continues for a few seconds longer until I see the TikTok logo and the sound effect that indicates that it has ended. I pass the new mother her phone back.

"Do you think he died?" she asks.

I frown. "Of course I think he died. You think there's a chance he didn't?"

"I don't know," she says. "I hope not."

I wheel my cart out of the room and later on I come back with three bottles of tropicamide and put the tasteless liquid in her tea and her food tray and her orange juice and the tiny syringes of breastmilk she has been pumping for her baby.

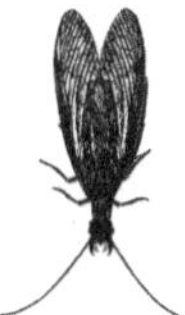

PART II
MANDIBLE

CHAPTER 15

I WANT PEOPLE TO WANT ME, BUT I WANT THEM to want me on my time. I want them when *I* want them. Sometimes, I want to curl up into a tight ball underneath an Alaskan Winter Coma Inducer comforter from Bed Bath & Beyond and imagine taking off pieces of myself, slicing off strips and shards. I think about how the flesh would come off. It would depend on what I used.

Or if you took a claw cracker and placed your ring finger in it. Cracked your finger back until it popped.

The kind they make for blue crabs, the tool that nobody from Maryland knows the actual name for because nobody here uses them.

Sometimes, I want to lay perfectly still and straight, arms to the side, elbows locked, and listen to the sickness move around inside of me. If I don't move at all, if I stay perfectly still, I don't feel the pain in my pelvic region. I don't feel the pain in my stomach.

But eventually I have to move.

I want to lay there and rot in my filth. But I'm not even just laying. I'm kinda planking, but on my back,

with my elbows locked at my sides and forearms straight up with my fists clenched and vibrating.

I poke my index and middle finger up straight at the ceiling, the popcorn ceiling. I press the middle knuckles of both fingers forward, arching the fingers, pressing out with the pads. I do this until it hurts.

I like to do a lot of things until they hurt.

People like to hurt me. They like to hurt me a lot with a lot of things and then they act as if it never happened. As if I don't exist. Because if I don't exist, I cannot be hurt.

I am starved for emotion. Starved for love. Starved for compassion.

But I am not even a thing. I am not even a thing, and hungry things eat, but because I am not a thing I cannot possibly feel hunger. There is a tusk that tears through the center of me. It is a tusk because it penetrates then hooks backwards into my spine. It hooks into the space between my L2 and L3 verte-brae. It bears my weight but it rips me in half and I am always split in two. I can never just be one thing, if I were to ever be a thing at all.

I like to do a lot of things until they aren't the same things. Like destroying the outside of some-thing. But also, the interior. Like agitating a bruise. Like rubbing the same spot until it's raw. Sticking the tip of a finger in a wound then corkscrewing it. A thin, red line spiderwebs out from the old wound. I cannot tell if the red line is directly underneath the skin, or right above it. The line is fresh and grows in the direction of my heart.

CHAPTER 16

I'm only 115 lbs soaking wet and my uterus is about to fall out, but somehow I manage to get all of the remaining Amiri Shirt parts out of the bathtub and into my suitcase, the one with the baggage tags from our girls trip to St. Thomas still attached to the handle because I haven't left the city since we went. He's much lighter than you'd think, but a lot of him went down my shower drain and garbage disposal.

When the pieces of Amiri Shirt went down the drain, some of the chunks stuck to the sides and I had to push them down with my fingers. I had to keep pushing the chunks down and they were squishy but rubbery, and somewhat resistant, like pieces of cheese and Panko breading stuck to the sides of an air fryer. There were tiny shards of bone too, little things like chunks of minced garlic.

I roll my suitcase down to the end of the parking lot and attempt to throw it in the dumpster, but it's hard for me to lift all the way up over the edge of the bin, so it kind of just sits there, stuck but not really stuck, held up by the weight of the

Amiri Shirt parts in it, sagging on each side of the dumpster edge.

When I was thirteen, I spent the summer at my Aunt Susan's house in Walnut Creek, a sprawling rancher with a barn and two spirited Appaloosas. I remember helping her unload the fifty pound alfalfa and grass mixtures off her truck, hay bales the size of my body that pulled me down when I tried to swing them off the pickup bed. The way the hay slumped and fell, slinking downward, barely held together by the twine it was wrapped in—the suitcase reminds me of this as it teeters on the edge of the dumpster, sides sagging sloppily.

I use both hands to push it over so that it lands at the bottom of the bin with a wet thud.

I go back to my apartment and wait for the red and blue lights to flash through my blinds but they never do. I wait for the abrasive knock at my door that never comes.

I make myself something to eat—Velveeta 3-½ minute mac and cheese and an orange soda because I love orange things—and turn on the TV for the latest episode of *The Whale*.

In this episode, the remaining contestants are out for a group date, aboard a yacht with the Whale. The girls lay sprawled across the deck on beach chairs with little more than suggestions of color to cover their nipples and sex. They listen to Top 40 and sip Dom Perignon.

I shovel mac and cheese into my mouth and struggle to swallow it down. I can feel the slimy noodles travel down my throat, feel it when they hit the wet bottom of my stomach. I can feel my body release stomach acids to process each swallow. I can feel the acids cut into me.

I push away my mac and cheese and pop a Klonopin, chase it with orange soda.

The camera cuts away to a close-up confessional shot of one of the contestants. She looks like a prettier version of John Boyega in the face. "Today, me and my baby get to spend some quality time together. Wooo!" She cheers and snaps her fingers. "OK, yeah, it's not like it's one-on-one time with me and the Whale, but look, this is good. The Whale will get to see me looking like this."

She rubs both hands down the curves of her body, starting at the sides of her breasts, coming in with her waist, expanding back out to slide across her hips and thighs, and finally, down to her calves where we cannot see because the camera does not pan down. The cutaway interview disintegrates and we are back on the yacht.

The thirty-foot tall curtain is there too, of course, the Whale—or what we must assume is the Whale—behind it. The way the vessel lilts to the side where the curtain is, it appears that whatever is behind the curtain on that side of the boat is extremely heavy. Because of this, we must assume that the Whale is heavy, and by the size of the curtain,

we must assume that the Whale is also tall. For something to weigh the yacht down, nearly capsizing it; for something to need a thirty-foot opaque curtain to cover the height of it, it has to be massive.

What could it possibly be? I wonder.

CHAPTER 17

DANEEN AND I ARE HAVING LUNCH AT THE
Popeyes on Broadway when the same man from the
night at Euphoria—not Amiri Shirt, who is currently
stuffed inside my suitcase in the dumpster, but the
man being arrested, the one yelling what sounded like,
you played, shordie, goddamn, you played like I ain't got a—
walks inside the restaurant. He's got a shirt on this
time, and those big, lumpy keloids that stretch across
his bald head like giant Madagascan millipedes.

"Did you ever end up fucking that guy?" Daneen
asks.

"Huh?" I don't know what she's talking about.

"From Euphoria. The one with the VIP section.
Y'all left together."

She wants to know about Amiri Shirt in my suitcase. "I don't even know, for real. I was fucked up."

"I don't know how," she says, sipping her fountain drink. "Those pills were bullshit."

I take a bite of my fried chicken sandwich, grind
it between my jaws and swallow. I follow the meat
with my mind as it travels down my esophagus. I

feel the morsel hit something and the pain starts again, searing my insides, blending up my center. I drop the sandwich on the table like it bit me.

"You good?" Daneen asks.

"Everybody keeps asking me that," I say, twirling my locs like I do when I think I'm cute, which is all the time. "I'm so tired of people asking me that."

Daneen dips a fry in ranch dressing. "You're making them worry, I guess."

The man with the keloids on his head approaches our table, puts his hands flat on it, leans over. "How y'all ladies doing?" he asks, smiling, and he's all radioactive yellow teeth and mildew yellow eyes.

Daneen backs into the corner of the booth.

"Fine," I say. "How about you?"

The man picks up my barely touched chicken sandwich and stuffs it in his mouth, starts chewing. Through a mouthful of chicken he says, "Goddamn! That shit good."

"What the fuck?" Daneen yelps.

Me, I just sit there, chilling. The man stays where he is, takes another bite.

Daneen is staring at me like I'm Captain Save-A-Hoe. "Aren't you gonna say something?"

I shrug.

"He snatched your whole lunch!"

The man leans in so that breadcrumbs and chicken fall from his mouth and hit my plastic food tray like little brown meteors. "Don't nobody care how the cake was baked!" he barks. "They just want a piece!"

"What the fuck?" Daneen yelps once more.

"They jehhh woannna peeeeshhhh!" He sprays more chicken pieces, empty yellow eyes, spit in the corners of his mouth forming cotton balls.

I roll my eyes, brush away a stray loc that has fallen in my face. "This isn't even the right context for that. He isn't using the expression correctly."

"Bake it, bitch!" the man shouts. "Bake it, bitch!"

Daneen throws her fountain drink at the man. Crushed ice and Pepsi splatters his white shirt dark brown. The way Daneen throws her drink, and where the man is standing, some of it hits me too. The man throws his hands above his head and runs out of the Popeyes on his tiptoes, screaming at the top of his lungs.

"I can't even," Daneen says.

I giggle a little.

"You just sat there," she says. "You just sat there and didn't do anything."

"I wasn't even hungry, to be honest," I say, and I'm not even lying like usual this time. Daneen grimaces. Blue flames tickle my uterine lining. My lymph nodes swell fat with poison. I pull at a hangnail until the pain in my abdomen subsides.

CHAPTER 18

Daneen and I mill about in the halls of L&D until a woman who looks like Frankenstein's monster arrives. She's covered in scars that look like her wounds were stitched back together with shoelaces. She's had no prenatal care and she tells us her name is Numi but we don't know if that's her real name. There's no way to know for sure. There's a man with her who doesn't give his name at all, the father, maybe. Their arms are blue with track marks, translucent like jellyfish. The guy is pretty far gone, chin hitting his chest, nodding while standing up. The woman is screaming; her eyes are bright, white globes, wet, and rolling around in her head like soft boiled eggs.

Daneen and I watch as the nurses wheel the woman in on the stretcher and immediately transfer her to the hospital bed. They start assessing her condition, arms and fingers jumping, rapidly moving around the room like ants. They check the woman's vital signs and stick an IV in her. They strap a fetal monitoring band around her gravid belly and she

throws up on one of the nurses shoulders. The vomit is a golden orange, the color of ambergris.

This woman is in hard labor but I can tell that she doesn't understand what's happening, that she didn't know she was pregnant, doesn't know she's about to have a baby.

I feel something mechanical tickle the inside of my cheek then slip back in place.

I watch nurse-ants skitter around the screaming junky woman. She pisses and shits on the bed and I can smell it from outside the curtain that poorly partitions the room. I lick the curtain and Daneen sucks her teeth.

"What the fuck, Jada?" she hisses.

Daneen and I watch until the woman drops a baby maybe sixteen or seventeen weeks old, nowhere near the age of viability, not even a micro-preemie. Intubation is pointless; a ventilator futile. No intervention.

One of the nurses carefully wraps the tiny package—which turns out to be a *her* and who is somehow still alive—and asks the man if he wants to see her, hold her.

"What?" He scratches his head. The movement is cartoonish.

"You're the father?"

"What?" he says again, not really asking. "Yeah."

"Would you like to hold her?" the nurse asks.

He accepts.

I feel the mechanical needle tickle once more, this time at the back of my throat.

The nurse holds the tiny package towards the man and unwraps her. The man screams. It's more like a shriek. Animal. The nurse jumps and pulls the tiny package back. The mother moans. The man snatches the mother's imitation MCM bag off the chair and bolts out of the room, pushing through the curtain and nearly knocking me over.

The mother sits up. "Where's my bag?" she asks.

The nurses don't know what to do.

"My bag. I need my bag. My bag. It's got my medicines in it. I need my medicines."

The mother tries to get out of the bed. The nurses try to keep her *in* the bed but it doesn't work.

"We can get you help," one says.

The mother gets a leg, and then two legs, over the side of the bed. "My medicines."

"We have medicine here. We can get you whatever you need."

The nurse holding the somehow-still-alive-baby says, "You could bleed to death."

Two of the nurses try to hold the woman down. They're not strong enough for her drug-strength. The mother runs out of the room too. It's quiet now, save for a few lonely beeps from the monitoring equipment.

"We don't even need to talk to Marcic, really," says one of the nurses. "Resuscitation is pointless."

Marcic is Dr. Marcic, the neonatologist. I slip past the rough thickness of the curtain partition so I'm closer to the tiny package.

"What do you mean?" another nurse asks. "We have to tell her something."

The room erupts. Arguing voices. Infighting and displacing blame. They don't know what to do. I use the opportunity to claim the tiny package and make my way to the lactation room. It's empty. I slide the curtain closed behind me. I unwrap the tiny package. She's still breathing, barely. Rasping.

I take off my scrub top and hold her to my chest. I place her tiny conehead between my breasts. She's warm. So warm. She dampens the edges of my bra with blood and amniotic fluid. The lactation room is so quiet. Her heartbeat is so fast. I find a clean receiving blanket and wrap her in it. Hold her closer to my chest. Her little head, no larger than a clementine. Ripples of movement in her tiny cheek against my skin. I try to speed up my heartbeat so it matches hers but it doesn't work, I only slow her down. I can feel her heart speed skip a bit then drain.

When she dies in my arms, it doesn't happen with a last breath or gasp or air suck. She just slows down. Her heartbeat, her pulls of breath, all of her. Like a cheap toy, her batteries drained to empty.

I put my scrub top back on and go back to the room where the nurses are still arguing about how to write up what happened.

"What are you doing?" asks one of the nurses. She looks at me like I materialized in front of her, like I just got here, and technically I did, but she doesn't know that. Only now, does she realize I'm in the room. She has no idea that I left with the tiny package and came back. How dare she act like she's in control.

"Just skin to skin." I hold out the tiny package with care. "Here."

The nurse snatches her from me. She looks at me differently now. There's a contained fear behind the native Baltimorean aggression in her eyes. The nurse looks at me and then looks at the other nurses. They look at each other. They look at me again. Then they look at each other.

One of them says, "I don't even know."

One of them makes wide eyes and wide eyebrows to indicate that she, too, doesn't even know.

"It's weird," says another.

They mumble and whisper. I don't mind. I'm used to people talking in front of me like I'm not able to hear them because they aren't looking at me, and because they aren't looking at me, they feel that I do not exist, and things that do not exist can not hear things to be offended by.

One of the nurses, short, with the kind of face that's pretty but also deceptively fat, says, "I don't have a problem with it."

"Oh, come on, Andrea," says the nurse who asked me what I was doing with the tiny package, the one who seems to be the ringleader of the group. I only know some of the nurses by name and I don't recognize this one. This alpha-nurse or whatever she thinks she is. "It's weird. She's weird."

The alpha-nurse who's name I do not know turns to me. "I'm sorry, but you are."

I can feel the look of surprise on my face because my eyebrows jump. "Huh?"

"Oh, come on, you know you are. You're always doing weird stuff like this."

The alpha-nurse stares at me, her mouth and nose hidden under a blue face mask, her eyes inscrutable under her protective face shield. I think she's pleading with me.

She places the tiny package in a plastic tub then turns to the nurse named Andrea. "You want to tell Marcic about this too?"

Andrea shrugs and looks at her Crocs.

"That's what I thought," says the alpha-nurse. She looks at me. "Why are you even here?"

"It's my j—"

"It's my job," she cuts me off, repeating my words in a mocking, cartoonish tone. Like she's deaf. Like she's retarded. Like she's implying I'm retarded. Like she doesn't know I could catch her in the Orleans Street garage and fuck her to death with a bottle of tropicamide. "You're not even supposed to show up until later. At the end. When they're about to leave. When it's car seat time."

I start to say something but stop. I don't have anything. The words float around my head. My brain is a red bowl of alphabet soup. What do I say? People will apologize to end confrontations. This is the easiest way. This is self preservation. But I can't. I can't do it. I can't apologize. If I do, it will destroy me. I didn't do anything wrong. I can't apologize when I didn't do anything wrong. I can't say sorry. I want this to end but I can't say it. I can't say sorry for something I didn't do. I didn't do anything.

"Fuck you, bitch!" I scream, walking backwards out of the room. "You got the wrong one!"

The alpha-nurse turns left, right, looking at the other nurses as if to say, I told you so. When I walk backwards out of the room, somehow I lift my right leg high enough for my Croc to catch on the heavy partition curtain, which somehow causes me to stumble into the curtain itself, ass first, my arms flailing outward, folding my body. The top portion of the curtain comes back and hits me on the shoulder blades, pushing me down to the floor. I fall on my face; my hair brushes the scuff marked tile.

I get to my hands and knees. Stand up. "You stupid bitches," I say, shaking my head and wiping my hands on my scrub pants. "You stupid, stupid bitches."

Before I leave the room I hear Andrea say, "Oh, dear."

CHAPTER 19

Sometimes at work, in between the patients and their stupid-ass babies with the tumescent, drying umbilical cords with the GPS tags on them, I like to pretend I'm in the passenger seat of a 1984 burgundy Ford Maya with peanut butter guts snorting lines of cocaine off the champagne tinted lenses of vintage Emmanuelle Kahn sunglasses. Skeletal fingers with glossy, manicured nails dealt five-card hands of Tonk. Automatic by the Pointer Sisters playing out of recessed ceiling speakers. Off-world guitar solos and brass-like synth sounds weaving together with pulsing bass. Neon windbreakers and such. Mint hues and pale pinks.

The Gold Coast in Chicago, Bal Harbor in Miami, Georgetown in D.C.

Neiman Marcus trips. Biscayne Bay. Luxury and refinement intertwined seamlessly. My body draped in ethereal dresses by Valentino. Chanel runway pieces. Men's suits from Tom Ford and Ermenegildo Zegna. A shoe sanctuary, lost art, like the Vatican, artistry showcased via the opulence of Christian

Louboutin and Jimmy Choo. Hermes Handbags. Fendi clutches beckon with an irresistible allure. Dior. Balenciaga. YSL.

I like to imagine that this is my life.

I'm not there yet but I'm getting there. Sometimes I have setbacks.

Just last month I was at the Howard Theater in D.C., dragged to a comedy show that Daneen insisted would be *worth it*. It was not.

The comedian headlining was a plastic-faced, uncanny valley-faced, mediocre garbage person by the name of Matt Rife. Surgery face without the surgery. Fleshy, pink Bakelite complexion. His whole schtick was just him ranting about being good looking in a disgusting Blaccent that made me feel like my uterus was going to fall out. He mouth-shitted about relationships and "you know how these girls be acting, y'all" with his generic crowd work, which was just him pointing out something obvious and acting shocked and appalled about it, portraying the image of some anti-PC, anti-woke warrior when he's the Burlington Coat Factory version of Dane Cook.

And Dane Cook is terrible!

But eventually I figured it out.

The loser's entire act was him being witty and charming. This fucking clown was just flirting with the audience. That's all.

The men didn't realize it.

But I saw that he wasn't communicating in the lens of *man to people*. He was communicating in the lens of *man to woman*. The topics, phrasing, and structured punchlines were something men don't get to see every day. But I see that shit everyday. This was just man on woman dialogue that women find completely normal and natural and oftentimes extremely off-putting and horrible because it's what they're confronted with whenever they're caught alone with men.

I realized then that I should probably make the time to kill Matt Rife.

But back to me at this Howard Theater and how fucking fine I looked. Because everybody knows a setback is a set up for a comeback.

CHAPTER 20

AFTER WORK, I GO TO THE DISPENSARY WITH Daneen even though I hate weed.

You have to go up to the door and press a screen and then they let you in. The door buzzes and we go inside. There's no one in front of us in line so we head to the concierge.

"Medical or adult use?" she asks us. The concierge is a light-skinned black woman with high cheekbones. Bald-headed.

Daneen says, "Adult use," and hands her driver's license to the woman without looking up from her phone.

"OK, great," the concierge says. The pink tip of her tongue darts out from between her lips, then retracts. "I need your ID too if you're going inside."

I realize she's talking to me so I hand her my driver's license. "Great," she says, typing into the computer. "Do you have accounts with us?"

"I do," Daneen says, then tilts her head towards me. "She doesn't."

The concierge looks at my mouth. "Do you wanna set up an account?"

"No," I say. "I'm just here with her."

She looks down at her keyboard and continues. "Yeah, but if you set up an account you can start accumulating your own points, and you can redeem those points for cash that can be used towards your next purchase. And we also send you tons of discounts and coupons when you sign up with us."

"No thanks. I'm just spectating."

"Huh?" She looks up at me. Once again, she doesn't make eye contact. Her eyes are drawn to my mouth, my lips, my chin. Wherever she is looking, it's below my eyes and above my neck. It's like she's making eye contact with another *me*, a shorter me, a smaller me, a less-than me. A *me* that exists directly below the surface behind a thin, diaphanous membrane.

"Spectating," I repeat myself. "I'm just here to watch."

The concierge doesn't laugh, doesn't snicker, doesn't smile. She slides our driver's licenses through a black card reader device, one by one, then hands them back to us. She presses the button that unlocks the next door and says, "Have a good night," without looking up from her keyboard.

We enter the adjacent room; a waiting area with cushioned chairs and a circular, glass coffee table that appear to be permanent fixtures, as well as additional folding chairs, brought out for the purpose of providing extra seating when the waiting area gets too packed. On the opposite side of the room is the door to the sales counter area. Barely anyone is in here today. There's me and Daneen and the security guard who stands in the corner scrolling through his phone. An orthodox Jewish man sits in one of the corner chairs. *Ella Mai* plays from a recessed speaker in the ceiling. That's it. That's all of us.

The door unlocks and swings open. "Joseph?" a voice calls out from behind the open door. The orthodox Jewish man stands up and crosses the threshold into the sales area. The door slams shut behind him.

Daneen types in her phone furiously. "What would I even cook?"

I don't know what she's talking about and I can't tell if she's talking to me or her phone, so I say nothing.

"But, like, seriously though," she says, her thumbs moving across the screen. "Like, I can't even."

She wants me to ask her what she's talking about. She wants me to ask so I do. "Cook for what?"

She lets out an exasperated sigh. "This one boy I'm talking to. It's his birthday. I asked him what he wanted. He said he wanted a home cooked meal. For me to cook for him. I don't cook."

"So don't," I say. "Why does it matter? Who the fuck is he?"

"I don't know. We're not serious-serious. Semi-exclusive, I guess. Whatever that means. Maybe a little bit. He took me to Dubai for my birthday. So I feel obligated, you know? To do something for the man."

Dubai, bitch. Daneen is so fucking lucky. All the time and always. Dubai is on my bucket list. So bad. And not because of Ferrari World or the sunset camel safaris. It's a well-known fact that Dubai uses slave labor. Like, the whole place, those beautiful skyscrapers, nightclubs, Ferrari World—built on the backs of slaves. The bodies of the slaves underneath the cement. In the walls. The Burj Khalifa, made entirely of bodies. A stacked body foundation.

They hold the laborers' passports hostage, they never let them leave. The conditions are terrible. And it's a city designed for rich people, by rich people. So it's not like they couldn't pay the laborers a decent wage, or maybe try not using slaves. They just don't. Because they don't have to. They can get away with it.

The entire place is completely ridiculous. The building of islands which rapidly sink, the fact that it isn't plumbed, the ridiculous gaudy scale of it all—it's just a giant playground for the rich and the fact that it's literally built on human misery and the destruction of the global ecosystem is just the rotten ass cherry on the shit sundae that is Dubai and I've never been more in love.

Daneen is so fucking lucky.

The door swings open again. "Daneen? Jada?" A stud with box braids and a septum piercing stands in the doorway. We head in her direction. She makes eye contact briefly and says, "Y'all at nine."

We walk into the sales floor area, which is a large room with an open space in the center. The perimeter of the space is lined with trade counters that the budtenders stand behind. Behind the budtenders, are rows of shelves with various cannabis accouterments stacked on them.

Daneen and I approach the counter with the number 9 on it. The budtender is an albino black man, young, or possibly old, it's kind of hard to tell. He has his hair in Pop Smoke braids; hair parted in the middle, tight cornrows that run down the sides of his head. The braids are thin. Red strips of skin stripe his scalp in between the rows of braided hair. His flesh looks inflamed. Flush.

"See your ID's one more time," he says, not making eye contact with either of us.

We hand him our driver's licenses. He looks at them but doesn't take them from us, then nods. We put our licenses back in our wallets, our wallets back in our purse. My wallet is a Florentine Zip Around Wristlet by Dooney and Bourke in the chestnut color. It only cost me $139, but I saved up for it, and I spent time shopping around online until I found the one I like. At first, I wanted to go with the natural color, which is like a burnt orange hue, but decided against it because it was too bright, too conspicuous. Daneen's wallet is an antique pink, lambskin Glycine by Christian Dior from their Miss Dior collection. The price tag on it is $560, although it's not like Daneen paid for it with her own money, I imagine.

The budtender looks at us, his eyes bouncing back and forth between Daneen's face and mine, then down at our chests, then quickly back up and away until his gaze settles at a spot that seems to be somewhere in between Daneen's head and mine, but not directly at either one of us. "Y'all already preorder?"

"No," says Daneen. "But I know what I want."

"OK, bet. What you getting?"

Daneen swipes at her phone. "I'll take two of the Evermore Sunset Octane carts, an eighth of the Tinselmint and an eighth of the G.M.O x Blackberry Cobbler."

The names sound interesting, like sweets, but they mean nothing to me because I don't smoke weed. I start feeling the tickle in my chest. It feels like the legs of an insect squirming inside of my solar plexus. Like thousands of tiny legs crawling. Whatever it is feels big, thick-bodied, like a cicada, or a dobsonfly. It feels like it's burrowing down.

The budtender says, "Bet. Be right back."

He leaves the counter and walks to a door that lets him into another room, which I assume is where they keep the weed stuff.

"You really don't look good, J." Daneen is staring at me.

"OK, bitch," I say. "Tell me I don't look good. What I need enemies for if I got you?"

"Not like that," she says. "You always look good, I just mean *good* like you don't look well. Like, it's giving sick. Not like you're not fine. You're still fine. You just look a little drained or something. I don't know. Forget it."

"You don't look all that great either, bitch."

Daneen rolls her eyes. "Yeah, OK, well, I'm the one who vacuumed a whole baby yesterday, least I have an excuse."

It takes a moment to register. "You're pregnant?"

"Was, bitch. *Was*. And thank goodness for that. Can't trap a bitch like me. I didn't even tell him."

"Tell who? The guy you were just texting?"

Daneen shrugs. "Hell no. Does it matter?"

"It matters to me!"

I feel like I'm on that ride at Six Flags that takes you straight up into the air and then drops you back down.

"Who I'm fucking matters to you?" Daneen squints one eye by raising her cheek muscle in that sarcastic-skeptical sort of way.

"No," I sputter. "Not saying that. But the fact that you were pregnant and didn't even tell me is crazy."

"It's not that serious. I can't get with a grown-ass man tryna get his life together, still tryna figure out what he wants to do. I'm not here to work on any projects. I'm complete. I don't have anything I have to work on. This clown was always talking about getting his CDL, Jada. A CDL? Fuck a CDL. I want a BBL. I'm tryna take first class trips to Dubai. I don't want to have a baby."

She goes back to her phone.

I didn't even know Daneen was spending that much time with the same man. How could she keep all of this from me?

The dobsonfly inside me has burrowed into my diaphragm, pulling off strips of my pericardium and left lung along with it as it makes its way down into my liver. It eats a small piece of my adrenal gland. It burrows deeper. The insect taps my pancreas.

Tap. Tap. Tap.

It tunnels through my stomach, then into my colon and small intestines. And then it stays there, legs rotating and twitching.

The albino budtender makes his way back to counter 9 with Daneen's order in a green basket. When he's inspecting the product to make sure the UPC codes on the cannabis packaging match the codes on his terminal, he has to use the camera on his phone to zoom in on the tiny numbers and expand the image, so he can see it. "I'm kinda blind and shit," he tells us, almost apologetically.

"Kind of blind?" asks Daneen.

"Yeah, like when I open my eyes I don't be seeing and shit."

Daneen swallows and tucks her bottom lip over her upper lip.

The thing inside me burrows.

The thing inside me pits.

Tunnels.

Its path diverts. It's going somewhere else. When it reaches my right Fallopian tube, it shrinks in size so that it can crawl along it until it reaches my left, where it begins to nibble at my ovary. It crawls back along the tube and when it reaches the center, it penetrates downward into my uterus.

"You don't want nothing?" the budtender asks me.

I bite my lip and shake my head, no.

"Oh ard. Well, your total $147."

Daneen takes out her antique pink, lambskin Glycine by Christian Dior from their Miss Dior collection and hands the budtender her debit card.

He takes out a credit card reader. "If you using a card I gotta round you up to $150 and give you back the change in cash. Cool?"

Daneen says it's fine and puts her card and PIN number in the machine. The budtender takes the card reader with the card still in it, then takes the card out and hands it back to Daneen. The dobsonfly inside my uterus reverts back to its original size, expanding and tearing into my endometrium.

I vomit black sickness all over counter 9.

"Jada, fuck!" Daneen steps back but it's too late. Black vomit hits her Jordan 1 Retro High OG Chicago Lost and Found's. "Ew!"

The black sludge pools on the glass display counter. It spreads. I see tiny insects moving in it. I rub my eyes and open them. I still see the insects.

The budtender is just standing there, watching this all play out from behind the counter. "Hey, I can't see shit, for real, so I ain't really sure what just happened, or what I'm supposed to do next. Y'all good?"

Daneen grabs her bag of weed stuffs from counter 9 and locks her elbow with mine. I turn my head and wipe my mouth off on my shoulder. Daneen ushers me out of the dispensary like a child. I turn back and see my insect vomit has begun to crawl up one of the budtender's arms. He doesn't seem to notice.

"Oh ard," says the albino budtender. "Y'all have a good one, I think."

CHAPTER 21

Dating is opening up four different apps and swiping and reading messages and trying not to give yourself an infected nerve in one of your bicuspids. Of these apps, my least favorite is Bumble. This is because Bumble requires women to make the first move by starting the conversation. It means men you match with can't just start messaging you crazy shit or sending pictures of their dick to you. It's supposed to help the power dynamics and encourage more respectful interactions.

But I never know what to say.

I'm attractive and I smell good but that doesn't translate through an app. I'm awkward. I don't know what I'm supposed to say.

Daneen tells me it doesn't matter what I say. Because they're men. That I could tell them that I believe Covid isn't real or that Black lives don't matter or that the moon landing was faked or that the core of the earth is the advanced civilization people really mean when they talk about Atlantis but don't know any better.

Or, even better, I can make them say those things, things that *they* don't believe. That I can have them believing those things if they think it means they'll get to fuck me. I can make them do things for me. I can make them do things for me and think they're doing it for themselves. Because they want to open me up and step inside of me. They want to fill me up. They'll do anything for it, *think* anything for it.

That's what I like, so that's what I do.

Jada, 25: hey sexy. what do you think about all those ancient Egyptian artifacts dating back to 7,000 B.C. that they found in the Grand Canyon?

Eric, 30: shit. lls. that shit crazy.

Jada, 25: you think that's crazy? what do you think is crazy about it?

Eric, 30: shit. idk. shit wild you feel me. ancient alien shit. you live by yourself?

Jada, 25: yeah. just me. you? no. i saw it says dog lover in your bio. that's stupid. animals belong outside.

Eric, 30: ;-) damn gorgeous. yeah I breed dogs, American Bullies. it's one of my side hustles. big money shit. you don't like dogs?

Jada, 25: i don't like them inside. if I came over to your place right now would you put your dogs away for me?

Eric, 30: shit. hell yeah gorgeous. no problem. you already. i got you. they already in the basement anyway.

Jada, 25: no I want them outside.

Eric, 30: shit lls.

Jada, 25: you don't want me to come?

Eric, 30: shit lls of course I do.

Jada, 25: then tell me what you'll do with your dogs.

Eric, 30: shit lls you crazy. i'll put em outside though.

Jada, 25: how many?

Eric, 30: how many what?

Jada, 25: how many dogs??

Eric, 30: shit like three?

Jada, 25: is it three or like three?

Eric, 30: nah nah nah it's three shordie my bad. so you smoke? drink?

Jada, 25: yeah I do all that. i do more than that. you're putting the dogs outside now?

Eric, 30: now? I ain't even send you my address. you not even on your way. why I'mma put them out now?

Jada, 25: i've never seen a man try to avoid some pussy this hard. you must be a litle boy. i don't mess with little boys.

Eric, 30: SHIT FUCK YOU MEAN. I AINT KNOW LITTLE ASS BOY. BRING THAT ASS OVER HERE AND WE GON SEE WHATS LITTLE. AINT NUFFIN LITTLE ON THIS SIDE. 13908 FULTON AVE, APT T2.

Jada, 25: ok lol he yelling now. you big mad?

Eric, 30: i'm just saying is you gon slide thru or nah?

Jada, 25: put your dogs outside now and I will.

Eric, 30: ok then.

Jada, 25: send a video of you putting them out.

Eric, 30: ?

Jada, 25: record that shit. send it to me. i'll slide and we can smoke and drink and get it in.

While I wait for this dumbass to put his dogs outside, this app and the others alert me that more men have swiped right on my profile. But who wouldn't? My profile is a picture of me and my name and my age and my sign (Gemini) and that's all.

In this picture, I am standing in front of the ocean with my back to the camera. I am wearing a strapless top which exposes my toned back and sunkissed shoulders. Even from the back, you can see the heaviness of my breasts by the sides which poke out. My hair hangs down my spine and terminates above the waistline of my jean shorts.

My ass is fat, thick. It pokes out too, two bubbles, a peach. The waist of my shorts stretch out and form a triangle at the center of my back because of it. The shorts are cut high. The bottoms of my ass cheeks hang out a bit, curves that hint at more substantial curvature. The backs of my thighs are smooth, brown, unblemished. Thick, in proportion to my ass. Muscular calves. I'm leaning forward slightly, my toes digging into the sand and holding me upright. Even the paleness of my heels in contrast to the rest of my body look good.

My phone goes off, this alert sounding different from the others. A longer, deeper vibrato. It's a media file. I open it.

In the video, a shirtless man, muscular and tatted up, corrals five dogs in a single file line through a narrow kitchen and out a screen door into a tiny backyard, really nothing more than a concrete pad with a chain link fence choked around it.

The dogs are upset. They do not look like outside dogs. Two of them cry while the other three just kind of sit there, confused, heads slightly cocked as if waiting to be instructed to perform a trick. One of the three whimpers.

Eric's voice says, "It's OK, babygirl. It's OK."

The camera pulls away and the image of the dogs in the backyard gets smaller. The screen door opens and closes. Back through the kitchen, the camera held in fist, moving shot of cheap tile floor.

He flips the camera so that it's his face filling up the screen, mostly just lips and nose.

"There?" he says. "Now you gonna come over here and put that shit on me or what?"

The video ends.

I message him back.

Jada, 25: you said you had 3 dogs.

Eric, 30: huh?

Jada, 25: don't huh me. that was 5 dogs.

Eric, 30: shit lls. they outside now it's cool

Jada, 25: no you lied. now I need you to kill one of those dogs.

Eric, 30: wtf

Jada, 25: serious

Eric, 30: you're fucking crazy. i'm not doing no type of shit. Fuck wrong with you.

I pull my scrubs off and place my phone on my desk, hit record. I get on my back on my bed. Stick my legs straight up in the air and peel my panties off slow. Peel them all the way up, so that my ass cheeks fall out, peel them past the backs of my knees and calves and around my ankles. I toss my panties behind me and click my heels together so that my ass cheeks open and close. I stop recording and put my panties back on, leave my scrubs off. The AC blowing makes my nipples hard. I crop the video so that it only shows me peel off the panties and start clapping. I hit send and wait.

My phone chimes. I pick it up and look at the screen.

Eric, 30: shit idc bout no crazy pussy too ccrazy not even worth it shordie lose my shit

It doesn't always work.

Sometimes I can't get them to do the things. Sometimes it takes little to no effort. I need to pick up some dope for the weekend. I check my neon orange pill bottle and count sixteen yellow Klonopins rattling around inside. That'll get me by until my appointment next week. But I'm all out of Percocet and I still need dope. Something to mix shit up.

I unmatch from Eric and text Toussaint to see if he's home.

CHAPTER 22

I LIKE TO PRETEND THAT I KNOW WHAT'S WRONG with me. I like to pretend I have Dissociative Identity Disorder and that my core identity began to suspect that something was amiss when she was 14 years old.

The first signs that something is wrong amount to blackouts and lost chunks of time. Saying things she doesn't remember saying, doing things she doesn't remember doing. Sometimes, she's recognized by a stranger out in public, someone she has no recollection of ever meeting before. Accountings of entire conversations that are completely alien to her.

At 16, our core identity—let's call her Imogen— gets referred to outside therapy because of problems at school. Imogen has bitten a classmate on more than one occasion. Biting is always cause for concern, not just because of how old Imogen is, but because biting is animalistic, indicative of something dark and primal underneath the surface of the teenage girl. Imogen is initially diagnosed with Bipolar I Disorder and PTSD, but upon further assessment, her doctors make the formal diagnosis of Dissociative Disorder Not Otherwise Specified.

In our senior year, we are formally diagnosed with DID, but by then we already know what time it is. At this point, our core identities are cognizant of each other and have been working together on improving our communication skills. We no longer fight to assert ourselves and have found our stations.

Which brings me to myself. My name is Jada. I am not the original identity, but it feels like I have been around for the longest. I keep everyone in check and do my best to keep the machine functioning smoothly.

I currently do most of the fronting.

Fronting is the process by which different identities take the wheel. This is what it feels like:

The identity fronting holds our sense of self, our sense of being. Our soul, if you're religious. When another identity takes control and starts fronting, we are changed into that identity. We do not *become* the identity doing the fronting. That is what we have been, what we always were, until the identity doing the fronting switches and then we were never that in the first place, and we can't imagine or remember what it would feel like to be this. Whatever I am, and whatever *I* is, becomes whoever is fronting. It is the feeling of watching our body move and do things that *we* can't control, that *I* can't control, yet thinking about it after the fact is like looking back through a fog, like amnesia, like a fugue state.

Imogen is our original identity. Until we graduated and moved out of our mother's house, she was the one fronting. This means that she was running things for the majority of our life, and the sudden change can only be attributed to our change in environment. We are unsure if Imogen's departure is permanent, or if she will come back someday and try to take the wheel back from us, but the general consensus from everyone with a dog in this fight, is that her staying away, and me staying in charge, seems like the best decision for everyone.

Matilda is a childlike identity who will tell you that she is six years old although she is actually three. She will say "gimme hug" and ask you if you've seen her tablet.

Mete is our second most prominent childlike identity. We believe that she has the emotional maturity of a 7-year-old, although her actual age is much older. She is closest to Matilda, and when Matilda can find her tablet, Mete enjoys watching Pinkfong YouTube videos with her. She also likes staying up late and watching movies and TV shows that are completely inappropriate for her, like *The Wire* and *For Colored Girls*. These shows are upsetting and give her nightmares.

Avi is a middle schooler whose only concern is getting into a nationally recognized private school, such as McDonough or Sidwell Friends. He believes that connections begin as early as elementary school, and that we have already run out of time when it comes to him. Imogen, myself, we've all explained to Avi that none of us can afford the $30,000 annual tuition.

Our oldest identity—not measured by time spent with us, but by his actual age—is Balthazar, a stoic man who claims to be a reincarnated 17th century Chaldean peasant. We are unsure whether we should believe him; our identities have been known to fabricate their backstories on occasion.

Tia is a lesser identity, a minor alter. She's rude, edgy and dark for no reason. If you asked me what she was into right now, I honestly couldn't tell you.

Farangis is a violent entity, age and gender unknown. Although they are aggressive and dangerous, they are not unpredictable, and because of this, we consider Farangis more of a nuisance than a hindrance or detriment. Measured quantities are something we can deal with as a team, and you know what to expect when you deal with Farangis.

Rick is an alter that I haven't interacted with much. I don't know much about him and it's been a long time since he made an appearance.

Hortense is the most emotionally mature alter in our system. At first, it was difficult to get a read on her. She kept herself isolated, closed off. But recently I've gotten to know a little more about her and she says her job is to hold on to our memories. She knows that is her purpose. To store and protect our memories. One thing I notice about her is that underneath her calm and put-together demeanor, she is hurting. Deeply. I think she is trying to figure out what she is supposed to do with all of us. She's like the mom of our group, I guess.

We also have an alter who will remain name-less, since their whole reason for existing is to per-secute and abuse the rest of us. This identity never fronts, and seems to serve no other purpose beyond causing harm.

CHAPTER 23

Toussaint lives on Guilford Ave in one of the Painted Ladies.

Back in 1998, Charles Village had a contest to see who had the best railing, best facade, best porch. Shit like that. So all the rowhouses are different colors. And different parts of the rowhouses are painted different colors, so you end up with this rainbow-colored block of houses. It's quite beautiful and something the city is known for.

Toussaint lives in one of these houses, the one with the emerald porch and electric purple columns with red accents. The main color of the house is this pale yellow, like something you'd see in a rehab facility. The windows are outlined in this nudibranch blue. Looking at his place without squinting when you walk up the steps is difficult.

On the way to Charles Village, Toussaint texts me that he left the keys outside for me in a bag of taralli and I need to let myself in. Then he sends me another text which is just the words *white girl booty* and the church emoji.

Fucking Toussaint.

I pull up a few houses down and parallel park, scraping the curb with my rims a few times before I get it because it's hard to see through the streaks of white on my windshield. I get out of the car and my insides feel OK at the moment. On Toussaint's painted porch, I find the bag of taralli, reach inside for the keys, and maybe a couple of the dry Italian crackers for myself—Gross! They're fennel flavored! Fucking Toussaint!—and go inside the house.

In the upstairs bedroom, Toussaint is sitting at the foot of the bed, butterball naked with his dick out, a flaccid, beige worm-thing. A tan turtlehead atop a dirty-blonde mound of bush. When he sees me, he tries to stand up, then decides against it. Two women lay across the California king, closer to the headboard. They're beautiful and they, too, are completely naked. Unopened bags of taralli—many different flavors, more than just fennel—are stacked three-high on top of the headboard.

Toussaint tries to stand up, hairless mole rat dick jiggling. Can't do it. Gives up.

"You ain't gotta get up, man," I tell him. "Just tell me where it is."

My tongue tastes like fennel now. Fucking Toussaint. I grit my teeth.

"That's why I fuck with you, J." He sounds like his tongue is too fat for his mouth. "Always tryna help a brotha out."

The reason I come to Toussaint is because he's the only one in the city you can count on for actual heroin. He's a user, not a dealer. For the most part. More so just a guy who has a really good plug that can get him heroin, rather than the mostly-fentanyl gel caps and red top vials that flood the city after every drought. He doesn't like fenty, likes getting high but doesn't want to die about it. Likes the opioid cotton ball cloud but the Oxy and Perks aren't strong enough for him, and besides, all of the pills are mostly fentanyl nowadays anyway.

"The shit," I say, taking out a folded stack of bills. "Where is it? Just tell me and I'll go weigh my three out."

Toussaint tries to stand up again. Can't. "Yeah, OK, but what you gonna put it in?"

He smiles mischievously like he's won this round, but we aren't playing any games so I don't know what the smile is for. "I can use this, it's cool," I say, peeling the cellophane wrapper off an empty pack of cigarettes I find on the dresser.

"Yeah, but it'll stick to the sides," he says, and gives me that sneaky grin again.

"It's fine."

He waves to where the connected bathroom is. I walk in and see the snack bag full of dope. It looks like Northern California beaches, jagged chunks of rock and sand.

"It's kinda wet this time," Toussaint yells from the bedroom. "You can hit it with the lactose if you want. Shits all there."

I see the bottle of lactose powder on the sink, the coffee grinder. Disregard it. See the loose playing

cards. I put an eight of clubs on the scale, tare the scale to zero. I scoop dope out of the bag using a folded ace of hearts, pour it onto the eight of clubs. It's not quite three grams, so I use the ace of hearts to scoop more dope onto the eight until the scale reads 3.0. I drop my shit in the cigarette cellophane, fold it once over because it's too fat to fold twice, put it in my bra.

The pain doesn't come back, but it feels like it is about to. At this point, we're intimate with each other, the pain and I. I know when she's coming. There's this anxious feeling, probably like what bipolar people feel in their manic states. I need to put the pain surge off or I'll never be able to drive home.

From the bathroom I say, "Is it cool if I do some before I leave?"

I wait for a bit but Toussaint doesn't say anything. I take that as my cue to carve up some lines of dope on the bathroom counter with one of the playing cards. I roll up a twenty and snort two thin lines of boy and then stand up straight. Straighten my back all the way out. Goddamn. It hits me in the sinuses.

"You good?" Toussaint calls out.

"Fine."

That soft, silly feeling in my front teeth hits first. It's not a numbing sensation, exactly. That's coke. It's more complicated than that. Then it's in my face and my chest and my spine and that good warmth in my lower back and sides and wherever my foul black kidneys are. My liver, pancreas, uterus—all of these systems soaked to rot, cancer metastasizing throughout my insides, creating tumors that look like topographical maps. The dope cleans all that. Cleans it right up. Ensconces me in lavender cotton ball softness. Violet. Ultraviolet.

It's giving love.

It's giving acceptance.

After the initial shock to my system, maybe like five minutes in, I remember that the expectation of a vengeful pain is still there, hiding, lurking in the shadows like a rabid raccoon.

I consider killing Toussaint but that's impractical on so many levels. The two women in his bed. The size of Toussaint himself. The cameras all throughout the house and the ones on the porch. And then I won't be able to get regular dope anymore. It'll be nothing but fent from the moment I bury my machete in his carotid artery.

Back in the bedroom, Toussaint is sitting at the edge of the California king, eyes not rolling in his skull as much, purple towel draped around his waist. At least now he's not completely naked.

"What you know about that white girl booty?" he says. He's patting the bare ass of the naked white girl passed out on his bed. Just tapping it, really. Light pats. Like he's reassuring himself that it's still there. "That's that white girl booty."

The girl isn't even thick. Her ass is as flat as an 8x11 and just as white too. I can see her blue vein lines.

"You don't really know nothing about that white girl booty, do ya?" Toussaint asks, still tapping lightly, still patting. "That's that good booty."

Pat pat pat. Tap tap tap.

The black girl on the other side of the bed yawns and flips her hair over her shoulder.

"Oh ard," Toussaint says, redirecting his attention to the black girl. "Got that black girl booty too. That's good booty. Got all types of booty. I ain't got a type. Not when it comes to booty. Not if it's good."

Pat pat pat. Tap tap tap.

The black girl isn't completely naked. She wears black spandex boy shorts, tight, up her ass crack, making her cheeks pop out like two separate entities. She's topless, laying on her stomach, heavy tits spread out to the sides. Toussaint starts patting her ass too.

Pat pat pat. Tap tap tap.

"I left the money on the sink," I say.

I hate when awkward or intense situations happen directly after I've insufflated my medicine. Completely blows my high, nullifies the painkiller aspect of the dope. I think about how I have a much better body than both of those girls, well, maybe not both, but definitely the white girl. My hair is better too. It's not Vidal Sassoon commercial or old copies of Jet Magazine, but it's better than the fried ends and cheap Yaki these bitches have. My skin looks better too. The girls don't look healthy. They're not full of vigor like I am. I'm glowing and I know it. The white girl is pale, yes, but she's pale like she's faded, like she used to be more of herself and this is what's left. And the black girl has this gray tinge to her. Like she's covered in ash but not ashy. I'm nothing like them. I have so much life in me.

"You wanna jump in?" Toussaint asks, watching me. I've been looking at myself, looking at the girls, looking at myself.

"I'm good," I say.

"Like I said, you don't know nothing about that white girl booty. Nothing about that black girl booty. Your loss. You played."

"You mind if I do a little more?"

"Sure," he says, and then, like a broken record, "it's kinda wet this time.You can hit it with the lactose if you want."

I go in the bathroom and begin the playing card ritual. Insufflate. Numb again. My eyes feel heavy, like my cheeks are full of chalk, like my sinuses are stuffed with something fluffy and textured. The thing about heroin—it's like a warm blanket. The *warmest* blanket, making you come to the realization that you've been cold your whole life. The trick to it is, you can't stay in that warm blanket for too long, because the longer you stay in it the colder the world gets while you're gone.

Like the fiends say, "Dope helps me with the pain...from tying my shoes! You feel me?"

I do another line and think about that piece of shit Matt Rife and how I want to kill him because not only was his act misogynistic, but he spoke disparagingly about Baltimore.

I let the dope wrap me in a cloud and transport me into the body of a mob boss. I'm sitting in a high back chair, leather upholstery. There's food and wine everywhere, charcuterie spread in front of me.

Napkin in my collar; fifty long, charcoal gray suit from Menizzi because I'm morbidly obese. Maybe there's a gravy stain or two on my white shirt with the monogrammed cuffs.

There is a young man seated across the table from me, some kind of foot soldier, maybe a Capo because he has managed to get an audience with me, the Don. "Boss," he says. "Thank you for seeing me. You have my gratitude."

"I don't want your gratitude," I say, guttural, Sardinian, throat singing voice, strong long island accent. "What I want is your loyalty."

"Oh, you got it, boss," he stammers. "You got it. There's no question about that."

I guillotine the mouth end of an Arturo Fuente Opus X. "To what do I owe the pleasure of this visit?"

"Well, boss," he says, "I just don't know if I'm the best fit for the job."

"Working for me?"

"No, no, of course not. I just mean this Baltimore job."

"Go on," I growl. A nervous energy invades the room like a gas leak.

"I know it's home base, but I can't grow here. I *thrive* outside the city. I'm an earner out of town. I make so much more money for you when I'm in Cincinnati or Detroit. Chicago. Anywhere but here."

This is when he notices my grip on the cigar is too strong, that I'm about to snap it in half. My hand is shaking. I've gone stop sign red in my fat yeasty face. I'm obviously about to lose my shit. My bodyguard has placed his hand at his hip. I turn to him, lift my chin slightly. His hand isn't on his sidearm yet, but it will be soon.

"Hey, hey, hey, boss, wait," the Capo pleads, starting to look like Matt Rife. "But overall, I think the reason for all that is because I'm retarded. And that's my fault, of course. Not yours. Really, it's a great city. America's greatest, if you ask me."

The silence in the room is tangible. You can hear a rat piss on a cotton ball. That type of nothing. Then I burst out laughing, belting out raucous barks and then my bodyguard is laughing and the Capo understands it's safe for him to laugh so he laughs as well, albeit a bit more nervously.

This goes on for a while, this outburst of men laughing from their diaphragms, barking like cane corsos.

"I love this guy!" I proclaim, clapping the Capo on the back and massaging his shoulder warmly.

"Ah, yeah boss," he says. I can see he's shaking a bit. "I love you too, heh."

I burst out laughing again and then my bodyguard is laughing and the Capo is laughing again too and everything melts back to me in the bedroom where Toussaint has passed out sitting up, his chin in his chest, drooling, and both of the girls are out too, snoring like vacuum cleaners, one of them sounding like she has COPD, so I leave his Painted Lady rowhouse and head back home to watch *The Whale*.

CHAPTER 24

ON THE NIGHT I KILL DANEEN, I CUT OFF MY fingerprints like Kevin Spacey's character in *Se7en*.

It doesn't work out for me the way it did in the movie.

I use my machete—the knife that isn't a knife—to do it and about halfway through the fingers on my left hand, I pass out on the bathroom floor like a twink and wake up in a smaller puddle of blood than I'm used to waking up in. Like there's less of me. Like I've started shrinking. Like the parasitic male anglerfish. Shooting cum until I'm empty. Empty of life. Completely devoid of blood. Completely devoid of cum. I realize I only made it to the middle finger before passing out so I rinse my hands in the sink and wrap the tips of my thumb, index and middle finger with Ace bandages. Blood seeps through and I realize I have more to worry about now than just fingerprints.

I take the machete and stuff it in my MCM bag, the large Liz shopper with the Cognac Visetos print.

Daneen lives with her mother in a single family home on Gerland Avenue. Her mother drives a Saab. Daneen drives a Volvo. Her father is no longer in the picture, but that's only because he's no longer alive. Daneen went to Garrison Forest. Elementary through high school, on some legacy-type shit. That's an all-girls school with a $37,000 annual tuition.

What I'm saying is that Daneen comes from money.

The thing about that, is that if you come from money or just have a lot of money in general, as long as you treat people all the time when you go out with them, it doesn't matter that you are better off than they are. Boast, brag, as long as you treat, tip, it's all good. They won't ever try to eat you. Just keep paying for shit. Just don't be talking about it if you aren't being about it.

Daneen is great at this. She always pays when we go out. Always. One of the many things I love about her. And she looks amazing, too.

See, Daneen is Instagram-beautiful. She's got these dick-sucking lips splashed across a face with hardly any buccal fat. Long, full mega-volume lashes, Natrelle tits, stiletto nails, BBL from Dr. Miami—so not the cheap kind that makes you look like an ant from the movie *A Bug's Life*. Daneen doesn't cheap out on anything. You can see her ass from the front, not just her hips, I mean. She's got that look, the one where you want to start stuffing things inside of her.

Filling her up.

"Why are you wearing gloves?" she asks.

I get into her Volvo and rub my gloved hands together like I'm cold. Fake a shiver. "Because it's cold as a whore out tonight."

"No it isn't. And why are you talking like that? You sound ridiculous. I picked this up for you at Saks. In case you don't have anything nice to wear tonight."

I can't believe she never told me she was pregnant. I can't believe she would keep something like that from me.

We take Frankford to the light at Radecke where Daneen hands me a black Fendi gift bag, the block letters of the brand name the same color as piss. Inside is a sheer Fendi bodysuit, the ones that look like what wrestlers wear, spread at the middle to show my cleavage. It had to cost her a fortune.

The way Daneen showers me with gifts while simultaneously assaulting my self-worth with her poison quips and verbal puncture wounds, she's like the male anglerfish, shooting me up with cum while draining my lifeforce and then dying on me, over and over and over again. My insides feel like a labyrinth. They feel like *the* Labyrinth. From the movie *Labyrinth* and David Bowie's massive, goblin king dick is stabbing me up in the kidneys and I might just throw up in Daneen's very reliable Volvo.

"Jada." Daneen is looking at me, then back to the road.

"What, Daneen," I groan.

"Something's wrong."

"No. Everything's right."

"The other day, at the dispensary, and just in general. And the gloves. And you don't even get your lashes or brows done anymore. It's giving broke, Jada. It's giving sick. It's giving unwell."

"I'm good," I assure her.

"You sure you're good, Jada?" Daneen asks, and this time, well, this time I just can't take being asked that question so I grab the steering wheel and swerve the car into the median strip. We're not going fast enough to jump it so we get caught on it. Daneen hits her head on the window, cracks the glass and blood lines the cracks in it. Neither of our airbags have deployed. I'm completely fine and my pelvic floor feels even finer, like it doesn't want to fall out of me.

I take out my machete—the knife that isn't a knife according to Daneen—and stab her in the chest with it. Her eyes do this thing where they bounce open wide, then click clack from side to side, then squint closed. Her eyes spring open again and she's trying to say something over the blood bubbles bursting on her lips but I'm twisting my knife that isn't a knife into her chest until it nicks her sternum so I pull back a little and experience resistance, like suction, like the machete is stuck in mud.

I finally get the blade out but it takes a lot of Daneen with it. Her body sags in the seat. Her head drops to the steering wheel and stays there. I check her pulse. There's nothing left, so I reach into the wound and start messing around in it. Just mixing it up and shit. Macaroni noises. I pull out my gloved hand, take off the glove, throw it out the window, stick my bare fingers back in Daneen.

Daneen's Volvo seesaws on the median strip. I get out of the car and smell something chemical. Like a pool. I pull open the driver's side door and undo Daneen's seat belt. I push her into the passenger seat and it's easy because she doesn't weigh much more than I do. I'm just folding up limbs and pushing.

It's giving broken sex doll.

It's giving CPR manikin.

I get behind the wheel and the car is still driveable, so once I've gotten it over the median I park against the curb and put the hazards on. I've really bled through the Ace bandages and my blood mixing up with Daneen's blood is making me wet. I grab Daneen's arm and drag it closer to me so that it hangs over the center console, her limp fingers pointing down at my lap. I pull down my leggings and panties to my knees, then use Daneen's dead fish hand to cup my entire pubic mound and I'm using her rapidly cooling fingers to scratch, dig, pump. I reach over and dip the fingers of my left hand in her machete wound, get my fingers nice and slippery. I rub on my clit directly for a little bit with bloody fingers until it's too intense. I take a break. Breathe. I slip one of Daneen's fingers, then two, inside of me. Grind down past the knuckles. I put my right hand on top of her hand, my left hand on top of the right and apply more pressure.

I use Daneen until I make myself cum and then get back on Radecke, riding it until it turns into Chesaco Ave, something metal dangling from the undercarriage of the Volvo, scraping the street. Whatever it is falls off when I make the sharp left on Weyburn, tumbling under the car and appearing in the rearview like a heap of metal entrails.

I pass Lucky Express on my left, a place I pretended to get food poisoning from once before. Daneen's just flopping in her seat.

The passenger seat belt warning is driving me crazy, but like really. Like I want to rip my ear lobes off and stuff them in my ear holes. Every ding is like a 10 gauge to the face. Then to my stomach. To my uterus. A continuous stabbing ache, amplified to sharp pulses by the seat belt alarm. It takes everything from me, and I almost lose control of Daneen's car, but it's a relatively new Volvo, so the steering wheel vibrates and the car recorrects itself.

Daneen flops to the side and kind of sinks into the seat and just stays there. Until she becomes part of it.

Waste of meat. Smooth-faced skin puppet.

I park in my reserved space and make it to my door, jingling my keys until I find the right one, when I remember that Daneen is the passenger seat. It's dark out, but I live in Rosedale Gardens so there's a dice game going on by the dumpster and some zombie-faced types milling about the apartment complex.

Fuck it.

I open the passenger door, drag Daneen out of the Volvo, and for some reason she seems heavier than before. She leaves a trail of blood on the cracked concrete as I drag her. One of her Louboutins slips off her heel and hangs on by the toe. The red bottom matches her blood droplets. I stare at it for a moment, wonder if anyone will notice. Unlikely.

This is Baltimore.

I take her up the stairs and we're back at my door. I fumble with the keys and throw her in the apartment. Before I go inside, I look to my left and right to see if anybody is watching me. To see if I've been made.

Nobody cares, really.

CHAPTER 25

In her 2018 album, "Dirty Computer," Janelle Monáe gave us the blueprint for an Afrofuturist feminist vision of how we should embody ourselves, one that says no to transhumanism and yes to embracing the messy, imperfect body as a powerful tool for telling our stories. While critics praised the album for its celebration of queer identity and Blackness, they contrasted it with her earlier work, as if the album wasn't an intensified expression of her commitment to deconstructing the concept of the human and breaking down the boundaries between human and machine. Janelle's idea of the *dirty computer* questions whether Donna J. Haraway's *cyborg theory* works for Black women, whose bodies have been treated as less than human for too long.

Let's take a look at Donna J. Haraway's *cyborg theory*. In Haraway's *Cyborg Manifesto*, we are presented with a radical reimagining of embodiment, and also of identity. Within the intricate tapestry of her theory, boundaries blur, and once rigid demarcations between humans and machines, nature and culture, or even between the sexes cease to exist. The cyborg, a symbol of convergence, emerges as a hybrid entity, melding organic and artificial components. This concept defies the confines of a singular, natural self and celebrates an ever-evolving, technology-infused identity. In Haraway's vision, the cyborg is an emblem of emancipation, a rallying cry for marginalized groups, as it offers the possibility of transcending the limitations imposed by conventional societal norms. Embracing intersectionality, her theory recognizes the complexity woven into identity, a tapestry of gender, race, class, and technology. It challenges the established order, destabilizing fixed gender roles and questioning the immutable human essence. In this way, her *cyborg theory* invites us to perceive human existence as an intricate mosaic, rather than a set of rigid, binary classifications.

It's funny how things that were once transgressive to us become mundane. Common. And then nothing.

Porn for example.

The earliest short films became targets for those campaigning against obscenity. One of the first to draw their ire was a 21-second clip featuring the first woman to appear before a Thomas Edison movie camera. This clip, starring Carmencita, a Spanish Vaudeville dancer, was among the earliest films that faced censorship.

People were scandalized by Carmencita's occasional tugs at the bottom of her skirt and the visible crinolines beneath it. Some accounts even suggest that the Newark Evening News reported an incident where a kinetoscope parlor in New Jersey had to pull the footage and replace it with "The Boxing Cats" after State Senator James A. Bradley complained that such an open display of ankles was inappropriate.

Fucking losers.

Anyway, the point is now people say shit like *earth porn* and *food porn*. Like it's nothing. It isn't transgressive. It isn't controversial. There's no scandal. But not too long ago, they were locking people up for pornography. And not too long before that, United States senators were filing formal complaints about ankle exposure. There's just too much sexy ankle!

Not on my watch.

Transgressive becomes mundane becomes common becomes nothing. This is the life cycle of *things*.

Growing up, it was an *absolutely no BET* household. I could never watch the channel. My grandmother was appalled by it. Especially the light-night program, *Uncut*.

My grandmother would wring her hands. "You won't be in here smoking weeds, watching the BET with the ass shaking and sickness and all that muskiness!"

One time, she came home early from church and caught me watching the *Bling Bling* music video and whipped me with a telephone cord. She whipped and she wailed and she strapped the cord against my flesh until my zest came off and I was less than.

What's funny is that shortly before she rotted to death in Harford Gardens from Parkinson's, I visited her and she told me that all she wanted before she died was some *bling*. Bling in her ears. Bling on her wrist. Bling on her fingers. She had only ever owned costume jewelry. All she wanted was some *real* bling.

She kept saying it, kept using the word. It was surreal.

Skin. Integument. Rind. Flesh. The duality of it.

Flesh precedes the body in different ways. On one hand, as highlighted by Alexander Weheliye, flesh serves as a temporal precursor to the body. The body, representing *legal personhood*, is forcefully brought into existence through violent acts against the flesh.

On the other hand, flesh proceeds from the body by being perpetually under the control of the body. The separation of body from flesh occurs, and concurrently, flesh undergoes sequential divisions imposed by the body. And the emergence of the body is directly linked to the disciplining of the flesh.

In order to determine who was correct—Janelle Monae or Donna Haraway—we are going to need to use the internet. Do a Google image search for Janelle Monae. Then do one for Donna Haraway. Based on physiognomy alone, we can determine that Janelle Monae was right.

PART III
WING

♂
♀
1cm

CHAPTER 26

THE NEXT MORNING, I WAVE GOODBYE TO Daneen—she's on the couch where Amiri Shirt sat before I deconstructed him—and go to work. I squeeze my eyes shut and wait for the SWAT team to jump out on me but they never do. Not even a pair of plainclothes cops.

The thing about things is that everybody's got one. I don't know what mine is. I'm still trying to figure it out.

One thing I've been into lately are male dobsonflies. The females are cool, I guess, but they don't really interest me so I haven't invested much energy in them.

Asian dobsonflies are the largest non-lepidopterans insect which makes them *really* cool. They have big seven-inch wingspans like lunar moths, big translucent floppy wings. They're terrible at flying. But the reason I like the males is because of their big, goofy mandibles. They're like two inches long. Heavy sclerotized things that they can't even eat with. Useless secondary sex characteristics on the males used by the females to evaluate whether they are going to let the males clap their cheeks or not.

Stupid.

And what's even stupider is that they make something for the females called a *nuptial gift*. A present they make out of themselves. Which is basically just a nutrient-rich mass of sperm that they shoot at the female dobsonfly. Not even to impregnate them. As a gift. A sperm ball gift. Like, here, eat this. It's your gift. Enjoy your gift.

Anglerfish, dobsonflies, Amiri Shirts, everyone—they're all just trying to shoot their cum at you.

When I get to the parking garage in front of Hopkins, I turn my car off and sit in it for a moment with my windows up, screaming the word *thusly*, again and again until I can no longer hit the *S* in the word and my voice feels like it's starting to peel apart.

I take the stairs to the second floor to put my belongings in my locker and Phil's in the break room, because *of course* he is. Sitting in the corner by himself. Sipping his cup of Rooibos tea. Phil. All by himself. All by himself, in here with me. He isn't looking at me, which is normal, but he isn't speaking either. He usually never shuts up.

I twirl my combination into the lock and pop the locker open. Throw my bag inside. "Hey, Phil," I say. "How about those Orioles?"

He doesn't respond but he flinches a little so I know he heard me.

I sit down across from him. "You know, Phil, I think you got me fucked up."

"Jada, come on, you—"

"Damnit, Phil!" I pound my fist on the table, make his tea jump and spill some of it. He backs up. "I was trying to express myself to you. I was trying to open up to you and you just cut me off, you just interrupt me like you don't even care that I'm speaking. Like I wasn't even speaking to you. Like you're not even listening to me. Like when I start talking, you immediately stop listening and start thinking about what you want to say next. That's not a good trait for a person to have, *Phil*. You gotta listen to people. Wait for them to complete their thought. Not just sit there thinking about yours. You know, it's important to feel heard, *Phil*. It's important to feel seen. This doesn't make me feel seen, *Phil*."

I realize that he's shaking, that each time I've said his name, I've punctuated it with an index finger to his chest. That I've been sitting here poking this grown man. Poking him so hard I can feel the caving indentation of his bird chest.

I don't know what to do so I stand up next to him and place my hands on his cheeks. I hold his face gently. Lovingly.

"Oh, Phil," I say, shaking my head, tenderly caressing him. "Phil, Phil, Phil. What are we gonna do?"

I boop him on the nose and that's when Phil starts crying.

The pain in my gut comes back with a vengeance and I double over and vomit out neon orange. Some of the vomit splashes Phil, but he's past the point of caring. He just keeps crying. It makes me sick. It's nauseating. It's visceral.

Phil's bawling exacerbates the pain, makes it unbearable. I want to make him stop but I feel like I'm about to faint. Everything is hot and wet. A splash of hot wet across my face. I have to get out of here.

"Phil, please," I gasp. "You gotta help me. Please."

He stops sobbing and looks at me with wet, red-rimmed eyes. "What?"

I dry heave. "I need help. You gotta get somebody."

He takes out his phone like he's about to dial 9-1-1.

"What the fuck, Phil! We're already at the hospital. Just get somebody. Get a doctor. Just get me somebody."

Phil wipes his eyes with his scrub top, gets up and runs out of the room screaming.

CHAPTER 27

On the way home from work, I get a text from a number with a *301* area code, which is the area code for the Greater Washington D.C. metro area, southern Maryland and rural western Maryland, rather than the Baltimore area codes of *410* or *443*. My iPhone suggests that it might be someone from Wet Systems Car Clinic, which, as far as I can remember, is not the name of the other mobile detailer I reached out to.

The text message states: $120. I can do it.

I don't have $120 but I text back anyway: OK cool. When can we set this up?

Wet Systems Car Clinic: Ready now if u r xoxo

Who the fuck types like this?

Another text message arrives almost immediately after the previous.

Wet Systems Car Clinic: Sorry. Tht was accident. Wrong person. Was texting you thinking it was them. My apologies, my queen.

Fucking weirdo. I should block him now. But I really need this bird shit cum off my windshield so I

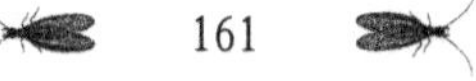

text back: Not available now. What about tomorrow during the work day? You can come to my job, there is a garage.

I see the three bubbles pop up, letting me know that he's typing something, or thinking about typing something.

WET SYSTEMS CAR CLINIC: Ard. Sounds good

CHAPTER 28

Here's the thing about getting Daneen off the couch and into the bathtub.

It's not easy. She's had some time to soften. Come undone.

It's like hauling bales of alfalfa.

It's like carrying a netted bag of Halo mandarins, a hole torn in the bag, fruit tumbling out.

It's like the rhino scene from *Ace Ventura: When Nature Calls*. Daneen's skin is the rhinoid decoy, her insides are Jim Carrey tumbling sweatily out the rhinoceros' puckered asshole.

Daneen has become part of the couch, the cushions part of Daneen. I dry swallow two Klonopin then step between her open legs, put my arms under her shoulders, lift her up. Her head tilts forward, chin hits chest. Her wet, matted, virgin hair sew-in taps my face, her hair on my lips, moist strands in my mouth. I pull her off the couch. It sounds like Velcro. It sounds like a T-shirt being torn apart.

Daneen is slush slipping through my fingers. Daneen is *fresas con crema*. Daneen is unfamiliar

soft parts collapsing and landing in heaps and puddles. Unfamiliar because these parts are never supposed to be seen outside of a person.

I drag my best friend across the living room;
wet pieces of Daneen leave a slug trail to the couch
like breadcrumbs to find our way back. I get her into
the tub, but it's more like I unceremoniously drop
her in there because I lose my grip on her right side
when her arm slides out of the socket, causing her
to tumble backwards into the bathtub with her legs
still sticking out of it. I push her legs over the side
and she's all the way in there now.

Daneen's right arm is squished between the tub
wall and her body. Her left arm hangs over the side
of the tub, her fingers curled into a claw. I remove
her dress and bra, her panties and her diamond ten-
nis necklace. I'm making a pile of these things that
I intend to shove under the sink when I hear what
sounds like hydraulic shop air.

That's when I see that Daneen's mouth has sprung
open. Like a frozen scream. Like it wasn't before. Logi-
cally, I should know that this can happen, that Daneen
is just settling. That she's going through changes. That
sometimes when your BFF is going through changes,
their body releases all kinds of gasses.

I fucked a mortuary assistant once. She had Tiffany blue hair and worked at Sol Levinson's funeral
home on Reisterstown Road. She told me over the
throwback hip hop music at Melba's Place that it's
like Thomas Lynch said—the dead are unremark-
able in ways that are hard to imagine.

I remember asking her if her corpses ever do anything interesting.

"What?" she had replied, incredulously. "What do you mean? They're corpses."

"Oh, come on," I said, touching her shoulder. "I mean, like, have you ever seen one move?"

"Oh," she said, laughing. "I mean, yeah, but no. It's not like you think. Occasionally they fart. That's just their body releasing gasses, though. The lids pop up though. We have to use eye caps on their eyes because the eyes don't stay closed."

"Eye caps?"

"Yeah," she said, taking a shot of Patron, "it's just like it sounds."

"So the eyes, or eyelids, I guess. They move. Sometimes."

She nodded. "Yeah. But if anything, it's the mouth that moves the most. Something like 90% of us die with our mouths open, and once it's open, it wants to stay open. The ones who die with their mouths closed only stay that way for so long. Their jaws snap open too. It's just how mouths work, I guess. So we gotta use string or pieces of plastic to keep them shut. Some people use needles. There's a huge debate over which method is the best among members of the mortuary community."

I threw back my shot, set the glass down. "Shit. That's a whole lot for a dead person."

"Well, it's not about them," she smiled. "It's about their loved ones. That's why they pay for it. For themselves. A person's eyes draw the most attention when they're alive, but when they die, their mouth draws the most attention."

Daneen's in the tub now, and that's good. There's not much going on with her eyes, but her mouth, cheeks; they're going through some kind of transformation, really drawing my attention. Her lips are sealed shut. She makes a low sound. Muffled. Something is in Daneen's mouth, making her cheeks poke out. Something *is* happening. Her cheeks tent outward. Daneen hums.

Squirming inside Daneen's mouth. It wiggles around, alive. A metal spike, a talon, something new, slips between Daneen's lips and over the lower lip, the tip of it nearly reaching her chin. The spike, talon, whatever it is twitches, rotating as if searching for something. It waggles. It points at me like an admonishing finger. It slips back between Daneen's lips. Her cheeks deflate and it's like it was never even there.

CHAPTER 29

I SNORT A THICK LINE OF DOPE OFF THE FORMICA countertop and watch a video on my phone about the future of research chemicals, how in a few years we'll be able to 3D print drugs in the privacy of our own home.

Some nerd with a Benjamin Franklin hairstyle says, "The future of biotechnology is bacteria capable of 3D printing chems. Imagine, your own chem dispenser!"

The video switches to a montage of images intended to terrify; viruses multiplying and faces melting off like in Indiana Jones. A voiceover says, "The concern is that individuals with nefarious purposes will use this technology to print viruses. Dr. Madelyn Ottone, head of the Virology and Pathogenesis department at the University of Maryland, claims to be able to do so."

A woman in a lab coat with rimless eyeglasses speaks. "We call it the Digital Biological Conversion Platform. DBCP. We are not very creative with names, but what we lack in imagination for acronyms, we more than make up for in results."

The doctor has an Italian accent. The image changes to some kind of machine while she continues speaking. "We can synthetically create an entire genome in our lab. We can artificially construct DNA chains. We use a chromatography column to di-deoxy nucleotides. Build the proteins. With a high enough precision nozzle, we are able to put it all together in a virus."

The image changes to male and female dobsonflies. There are many. They crawl on top of each other and flip over on their backs revealing tiny legs that twitch like the perpetual movement mechanism of a Rolex Submariner. The camera zooms in. It's all legs.

The name of the Youtube channel is Curry-HouseClips. I click the *like* and *subscribe* buttons.

CHAPTER 30

DANEEN'S IN THE BATHTUB TALKING SHIT ABOUT how terrible I am at world-building. I can hear her all the way in the living room.

"You gotta come up with something better than that," she says. Now that decomposition has set in, the sound of her voice is like the smell of one of those living museums in colonial Williamsburg, where the staff dresses up like Thomas Jefferson and they show you how to churn butter. "You wanna do something elaborate, girl, you can't just kill your coworker. Whether you do that shit in a public way or a sneaky way, that's boring. Terrible world-building."

"I fucking *hate* Phil!" I press my thumbs into my sides and massage whatever organs are metastasizing in there. "I mean, the hate I have for that fucker is visceral. I can feel it in my teeth.

"Like I said," Daneen squeezes water from a washrag. She lets it drip down between her deflated breasts. "You're just not good at world-building. It has to be bigger than that."

Daneen tells me that I should bring a bomb to Hopkins on Tuesday. Something with fertilizer. And lots and lots of gasoline and styrofoam. That I can get styrofoam from the mailroom downstairs where they keep it for fragile shipments. That I owe her that.

At the very least.

I tell her that this is silly because there is no reason for such extreme measures. There's so many things at the hospital that can't be traced. The things nobody cares about. The ones nobody keeps an inventory count of so they're always running out and having to pay overnight shipping to get when they need it last minute.

The ophthalmology wing works with tropicamide, for instance. They have medicine cabinets full of the stuff; little cylindrical white bottles, stacked on top of each other and ready to go. I can simply empty a couple of droppers into the communal Keurig unit's water tank in the NICU and just...wait.

The shiny new mandibles on each side of my friend's sunken face stretch out horizontally and twitch. Daneen deploys her haustellum, spitting it out like she's still not used to it yet, which she isn't. The bulbous end of it probes the air and opens up; a wet, pink corolla, shaking violently, petals floating to the ground.

I check TikTok. It's the one social media platform I don't pay as much attention to. Initially I resisted, mostly because I didn't think I could handle the pressure of maintaining a new social media platform but eventually I succumbed, in the same way I did with Instagram and Snapchat(RIP).

TikTok is interesting because it has a setting on it where you can see who's been viewing your profile. The downside is that everyone else can see if *you've* been viewing *their* profiles if you have that setting turned on. It's invasive, but it's hard to resist being able to see who cares about you.

I don't really pay attention to what anybody else does on TikTok. I like to watch the ones that show ex-junkies during their junky stage as the pictures of the user get progressively worse, with *Breaking the Habit* playing in the background until eventually arriving at an image of the user, now drug-free with a mouth full of veneers, their skin free of wounds, and a caption at the bottom that says: *the most common way that people give up their power is by thinking they don't have any.* I like to watch them because when they get to the part where the user is hobbled, shoulders hunched over and head angled down, their eyes are looking up at the camera, and there's nothing in their eyes at all, so it's like they're looking at only you.

And their lower lips are always turned down. Smug. The line of their mouth looks like the letter L laid on its side. Like it's your fault this happened to them.

I put my phone away and try to dry swallow a Klonopin, but it gets caught in the back of my throat—this has been happening a lot lately—so I put my head in the sink and guzzle metallic-tasting water from the faucet until I get it down. I feel the

Klonopin dig a ground nest in my stomach lining. When I look in the mirror, I see the water has left my mouth and chin slick and gray. I wipe my face with the back of my arm.

Daneen snaps one of her mandibles, I mean *really* snaps it, like she's snapping her fingers. The sound is metal on metal. Once again I bring up the Keurig machine. The tropicamide. Daneen tells me this is a terrible idea because not everyone drinks coffee.

CHAPTER 31

At the beginning of our shift, the nurses and the attending physician and the lactation consultants and everybody working on the 8th floor and I all get together behind the front desk and have a huddle where we go over our patients for the day.

If the patient is a new mother, they have to get through me. They have to listen to my whole routine. For the baby's safety of course. If it isn't their first time, I just have to make sure their car seats are functional. They don't get the whole speech. I have a lot of downtime when the patients aren't first time mothers. I like to pretend I'm a contestant on *The Whale*. And it's fine because the anesthesiologists only do about eight minutes of actual work before spending the rest of the time playing *Candy Crush* or checking their parlays on *Draft Kings* and they make close to $400,000 annually so I feel like my behavior is acceptable.

In my own version of it, the one that's all mine, *The Whale* is a reality TV dating show where an unidentified individual known only as the Whale, is concealed inside a steel drum with silicone umbilicals running from it. The tubing connects to cylindrical vats of neon green amnio. The contestants (of which I am one) go through a series of tests or challenges to prove how invested they are in the Whale, ranging from blennokinetic enemas to blood eagle torture.

And then I remember standing in a cemetery. Druid Ridge Cemetery. It's raining. The light, sprinkly kind that feels like it's coming up from the ground.

On the day my mom died, I stayed in my bedroom, refusing to go with the rest of the family to the hospital, and see her one last time before they buried her in the cemetery at Old Court and Reisterstown Road. I made excuses that I didn't want to remember her like *this*, whatever *this* was.

But this was a lie.

The reason I didn't attend is because death deserves nothing. It doesn't count. I wasn't going to start speaking her name differently. She would still be her. I would never let death take that. Death is just a pause.

I know this. I know that I did not attend. I know that it has already happened. And yet, I have the memory somehow, of me at my mother's funeral. My uncles are there, dressed in black. My father is not there because he is a phantom even in my dreams. The rest of the bodies blur together in black and gray smears. Watercolor drips. Like looking through black jelly.

They lower the coffin into the ground with pulleys that creak as they turn. It sounds like the intro to that *Trillville* song. Small clumps of soil roll off the sides of the coffin.

Here it is, hoe, what's up.

The pastor is saying something and the pastor is Matt Rife, but less than. The pastor is Matt Rife but a large portion of his face is gone. The jaw hangs diagonally, dislodged. Ropey meat connects the upper portion of the face to the hanging jaw. The tendons and skin look like lengths of red and black speaker wire.

"You can catch me at the funeral," he says, torn jaw flopping lazily. "But I won't be going to the bypass."

He waits as if to get a reaction. When none is given, I shout out, "I think you mean *repass*."

"What's that?" he says, cupping a hand around his ear, the one he still possesses on the undamaged side of his head.

"Repass," I repeat myself, cupping both of my hands around my mouth to amplify my voice. We're not even that far away from each other. "You meant *repass*. Right?"

"Shitttttttt," he says, drawing out the word until it hangs like a Slinky suspended in mid-air. "I said what I meant and I meant what I said. And I meant *bypass*. Because a motherfucker finna bypass all that shit!"

Cue the canned laughter.

CHAPTER 32

I HAVE SEVENTEEN MISSED CALLS WHEN I WAKE up on the couch, my scrubs slightly damp from sitting where Daneen once sat before I put her in the bathtub. My thighs are sticky, the inner and outer of them. I feel her in my cracks and crevices, in my folds. Daneen. Fifteen of the missed calls are various numbers coming from Hopkins. I can tell by the first three digits. 9-5-5. The other two calls are from a number I don't know, 4-1-0 area code and the next three digits—all sevens—remind me of something government related.

I pop a Klonopin and call back the number because I hope it's the police.

A woman answers. "Northern District."

The police! I was right, and once again I am in a game and in this game I am already in the lead by one point. "Somebody called me?" I say, and I say it like Daneen would, with a question mark at the end.

"OK. Who are you?"

I give the woman my name and wait when she puts me on hold. The hold music is the same as the

hold music at Hopkins. Everything in this city is connected.

A new voice, a man's, gets on the phone. "Hi. Yes, Jada. Thanks for calling me back. Yeah, that's terrific. So my name is Detective Thomas Wright, OK? And I'm wondering if you could help me out here."

"I don't know," I say.

"You don't know?"

"Yeah, I don't know. I don't know if I can help you."

"I haven't even told you what I need help with."

"That doesn't change anything," I say, knocking things off the counters as I pace around the kitchen.

The detective sucks air back through his nose and exhales a sigh. "How's that, Jada? You don't know if you can help me? Like *me* specifically? You could help if it was somebody else doing the asking?"

"It's not like that. I don't fuck with the police, for starters. But like, also, I'm kinda busy right now?" and I say the word *now* with a question mark on it. "So to be honest with you it's a combination of both of those things, but also, really, I've been all over the place lately and I feel like I'm not gonna come off my best."

"I don't need you to be your best, Jada," he says. "I just need you to answer a few questions for me."

"I really think I'd be my best at another time."

"You called me."

"Am I under arrest?" I ask him.

"Over the phone?"

"Right," I say. "That does sound retarded. OK. What's up?"

"Daneen Mosley. You work together. You're friends?"

"That sounds like a question, except it's not really a question. You're saying something we both know already."

"OK," he says. "Right. So, can you tell me about the last time you saw her?"

"Yeah. Definitely."

"Well, can you tell me? When that was?"

"Sure, I guess."

I don't say shit.

"You still there, Jada?"

"Look. I can answer your stupid-ass questions but you gotta answer mine."

"OK," he says. "Whatever. Shoot."

"Did you know that 40% of police commit domestic abuse? It's a fact. I saw it on Reddit and Reddit is always completely factual. All of you, just beating the shit out of your wives. Just a big wife-beating party. You just toss em all around the room like laundry bags. Sacks of autumn leaves. Big yard bags. You just toss em around. Beat the shit out of em. That's what you do, Thomas? You beat the shit out of your wife."

Now it's his turn to let the line go dead for a bit.

"I don't have a wife," he says, frustrated. "And I'd never lay a hand on my husband."

"Oooooo, husband," I say. "How progressive. How contemporary. I bet you beat your gay-ass husband."

"When's the last time you saw Daneen?" he asks, the tone of his voice different now.

It's giving dry ice.

It's giving white room torture.

I chuckle and tell him that the last time I saw Daneen outside of work was when we went out to Euphoria like we always do, and that we sat at tables facilitated by fuck boys, got free Casamigos that we mixed with most-likely-not-MDMA molly of unfamiliar origin and then Daneen must have dropped me off like usual because she wasn't at my place when I woke up, and that later on that week we ate Popeyes on our lunch break and went to the dispensary so Daneen could buy weed and that I haven't heard from her since.

We both let the silence on the line linger this time. Let it grow fat.

"Jada," he says. "Why don't you come in sometime? I think you could help us find Daneen. That's what we all want. Daneen's parents are devastated right now. What do you say? Come by the station in about an hour."

"No, I don't think so," I say.

"OK, no pressure. Later this afternoon? Tonight? I'll be at the station until 7:00 p.m. You're not in any trouble, Jada. We just need help finding Daneen."

"I'll think about it," I tell him, before hanging up the phone.

CHAPTER 33

ARLINGTON FAWOLE IN HR HAS ONCE AGAIN RE-quested that I come in. What he does not know is that he and I are in the middle of a duel, a game of sorts, with very specific rules that only I know. In this game, I have nothing to lose, and judging by the *Best Dad Ever* mug and the framed pictures of vacant-eyed family members on his desk, Arlington has everything to lose.

"Jada," he says. "This has to stop."

I sit in front of his desk cross legged, my legs folded up in the chair, knees tucked under my chin, scrubs pulled up revealing my dirty ankles. With the bathtub always being occupied and sink baths my only option, it's been a minute since I've been able to wash anything below my waist. This is me making the first move, filling up his office with my musty miasma.

"Stop what, *Arlington*?" I enunciate every sylla-ble in his name like I'm slow.

"You're making people feel unsafe."

"Unsafe?" I reiterate. "Unsafe. What does that even mean?"

"Like they don't want to come to work if you're going to be there."

"Who is *they*?"

"Everyone, Jada," he groans. "Everyone."

"Not Daneen," I counter. "Daneen likes me."

"Daneen hasn't been to work in days," he says. "Nobody's heard from her. We've been trying to contact her with no luck. And that's besides the point."

"I don't know, man, that's my whole point."

Arlington takes off his glasses and pinches the bridge of his nose. "We have to take appropriate corrective action. We've tried verbal reprimands. We've tried written. The only option we have left before termination is suspension."

"Suspension?" I say. "Like in school?"

"If you like," he says, rubbing his eyes.

"Am I still gonna get paid during the suspension?"

"No. It would be unpaid."

I uncross my legs, put them on the floor, sit back, cross my arms, sneer. "That's gay."

His eyelids explode open, his eyeballs bulge out like a fish. "You can't say that!"

"What do you mean I can't say that? I just said it. Obviously I can say that."

He's stammering and stuttering but he's not saying anything. Just sounds. He's getting himself all worked up, I can smell it. His face is swelling and so are my insides. I'm too small to keep this all in.

I feel something rupture in my lower intestines and spread coldly through my gut.

I cut him off and say in a low voice, "I can take a shit on your desk, *right now*, and there's nothing you can do about it."

"What?"

I rise. "I said—"

I get up on his desk. "That I—"

I'm on my knees and then I stand up again. "Can take—"

I pull my scrubs and panties down and squat, my ass in his face. I push until I feel the veins in my forehead bulge out and thump. "A shit on your desk right now—"

He backs up, the back of his chair smashing into the bookshelf behind him. "And there's nothing you can do about it."

And then I do it.

"What the fuck?" he screams. Then his mask slips completely. "You stupid bitch! Oh God! What's wrong with you?"

It hits his desk with a *poomp* and the room is all sulfur and I need more fiber in my diet.

He's screaming something in a high-pitched voice at me. I grab the stack of written reprimand templates from his desk and wipe my ass with it. I ball up the shitty papers and toss them over my shoulder at him. Grab some more.

I pull up my panties, leggings. Jump off the table. I'm going through the filing cabinet with

everybody's personal information who works in the
NICU, and by the time I find Phil's folder, Arlington has got his shit together enough to call security,
so I run out of the office and don't stop running until
I make it to my car.

CHAPTER 34

I EXPECT DETECTIVE WRIGHT TO BE STOPPING BY my place soon, so after I puke into the sink it's time to get rid of Daneen's Volvo.

Daneen's Volvo is an S90, and I know this not because I see it on the rear of the vehicle as I approach it, but because Daneen makes sure to tell everybody what type of car she drives.

"They're the safest cars," she likes to say. "That's why I got one."

The reason Daneen has a Volvo is because her parents bought it for her. They figure it's the safest car and parents love safety when it comes to their children. She likes to tell this story about how the *large animal detection system* saved her life.

"So I was driving on Cold Spring, right?" she says. "And this huge deer jumped out in front of me, but it ended up being totally fine, because the flashing warning and the brakes activated *before* I could even react, and that saved my life. I'm not saying I'm not a good driver, I'm saying that if you were in the same situation and your car didn't have the *large animal detection system*, you might be in some trouble."

I press the push-to-start and Daneen's stupid safety-mobile comes to life. The leather interior is soft, cold. I kinda sink into the seat. The engine purrs, and I guess I start thinking about how it's a pretty cool car, actually. The screen in the dash is huge. All types of settings and presets. Glowing buttons. LED lights.

It's really not bad at all.

The parking lot of the apartment complex is almost empty. People at work. But not Daneen. Daneen won't have to go back to work anytime soon. Lucky Daneen. She never has to work again. She can just be pretty Daneen.

And then it hits me.

Burning.

Stinging.

Vibrating.

Pulling.

Soft, grayish cement guts, hardening into concrete inside of me. Sharp, rough edges hitting everything in my abdomen. Pain coming in waves. Uterine contractions, like something is trying to push me inside out. I can feel my ovaries throb with my heartbeat. Time passing strangely like this one moment is the longest thing I've ever done.

I don't know how long I sit in the car before I leave the apartment complex, but I get on the road eventually, start making my way to the Eastside. The way I see it, I can park Daneen's car somewhere

Down Da Hill, maybe leave it on Curley or Linwood, windows down, doors unlocked. The city would take care of it. Like the ocean. I would turn Daneen's Volvo into a whale fall. Big marine mammals dying and falling to the bottom of the ocean, turning into vast ecosystems for other life to feed on and build their homes in.

That's what will happen to the car.

By the time the police find it, if they ever do, it will be a literal shell of its former self, and that's literal in the *literal* sense of the word, as in everything from the catalytic converter to the windshield wipers will be stripped until it's nothing but German engineered chassis, so I take the Pulaski Highway to Linwood, make a right and take it all the way up until I hit Monument Street, then bust a right and put the car in park at the corner of North Curley.

That's where I leave Daneen's Volvo.

It's not even late and nobody is outside. I never see Baltimore like this. It's beautiful.

I walk down Linwood until I reach Jefferson, wait for the light, then cross the street. I take Jefferson until I get to Ellwood Park. I pass the soccer field on my right, then a basketball court with the hoops removed from the backboards. Goose shit all over the walking path.

I went to a white trash wedding here once. The centerpieces at each table were vases with betta fish in them. They were those live aquaponic situations, the planters on top with the fish habitats at the bottom, the color of the gravel coordinating with the wedding party colors. They were supposed to be parting gifts, goody bags or whatever. It didn't make sense because there were ten or so tables, each with six or more people seated at them, and only one betta in one vase for each table. Quite a few people were going to leave empty handed.

But the betta never made it that far.

I remember sitting in my mint-hued bridesmaid dress, sloppy from old fashions, legs spread out, complaining to no one. "They don't even muddle the cherries. I didn't see them muddle shit. Did you?"

The white trash children of the white trash wedding guests had brought all of the centerpieces to one table, circling around it.

"You do it, Bernard!" one of the children said, face filthy and hair knotted.

Another filthy child pushed her back. "What do I even pick em up with?"

I killed my watered-down old fashion and stood up. "What are you little dickheads trying to do?" I asked.

"Ha!" said the little girl, pointing at the boy. "She called you a dickhead."

"I called all of you dickheads," I said, going around the table with my index finger and briefly coming to rest in each of their directions, making sure they knew that each and every one of them were dickheads.

The girl walked towards me, palms up. "We're trying to put these fish all in the same vase. They're fighting fish. Did you know that? If you put them in the same tank they'll kill each other, the dummies. So we're gonna put them all in the same vase."

I stroked my chin. "That's a great fucking idea."

The little girl held her hands out, palms up. "But how do we get them out?"

"You could pour them out. Just pour most of the water out first so you don't overflow the vase. Then plop them right in there. Easy."

The little girl raised her eyebrows. Bernard looked impressed. The rest of the trash children had lost interest and were swarming the empty tables, drinking the alcohol backwash at the bottom of the discarded drink glasses left by the adults before they migrated to dry hump-dancing on the basketball court.

Bernard and the little girl got to dumping out the centerpiece vases, pulling the aquatic plants out like corks and pouring out the water until the bettas almost tipped over the lips of the glass. They had about eight vases with an inch or two of water left in each one; brightly colored fish with vermillion and chartreuse feathered fins flopping at the bottom. They left one vase with the water and an electric blue betta swimming around in it, the aquatic plant already pulled out of the top.

They started dumping the other bettas in this one.

The fish only poked around each other for a bit before turning into a blur of color. Water jerking around, splashing up the glass. Then muddy brown, frothy spume, circling around the vase like a drain.

"Holy shit," said the little girl.

Bernard started to cry or something, I don't really remember.

I make it out of the park and I'm on Orleans. Brick on brick on brick on brick. Rowhouse after rowhouse until I sit down on a bench at the corner of Orleans and Lakewood. This part of the city becomes redundant if you look at it the wrong way. The wrong way, is thinking that each of these feats of architectural greatness are identical.

There are federals. They are symmetrical and have decorative shit like cornices. There's Greek. Neoclassical-type. You see a lot of those in Mt. Vernon. Some people think they are kinda plain, but I think they are scientific. You got Italianates, three-stories, six narrow windows at the top, red brick, stained glass doors. Bowfront houses—brown brick with white marble steps, days spent scrubbing those steps for my grandmother. Little affordable two-story, two-bays. Peeling white brick. New trees. Old trees.

I set up an Uber to take me back home, and before I can confirm *method of payment*, the 50 caliber BMG hits me in the belly.

It starts with a stab and a pinch deep down in my pelvis, then flashes of lightning shoot down into my vagina. And it's heavy, oh God is it heavy, and my whole belly is bloated and distended, and it drags me down, and my lower back is pulling me down, and everything is heavy. When it gets to my legs it's like cold hands that inch further down until they're trying to break my kneecaps, and they take their time. It's like a screwdriver in my cervix. I can't think I

can't talk I can't move and there are whole civiliza-
tions being destroyed inside of me. Shredded strands
and strips of pulled pork, like my abdomen is full of
fiberglass, poison swarming, teeming, ripping, tearing, stabbing, asshole lightning, pussy lightning,
lightning down my legs to the tips of my toes like if
I ever try to stand up again I will tear myself in half,
and there will be thin strands of ropy muscle that
will still connect me but it will not be enough to hold
me together. Like my midsection is being crushed in
the hand of a greek god, heaviness, throbbing, taking
my breath away, takes me to the floor, to the cement
floor, dirty sidewalk vials and used condoms, take
me to the cold touch of it, put my cheek down on the
fuzzy sidewalk, just a little bit, just so much pain, no
matter what, all the time, forever, and that's when my
phone starts aggressively vibrating, letting me know
that my Uber driver has arrived.

CHAPTER 35

DANEEN'S BACK TO SAYING HOW IF I KILL PHIL IT will cause my character arc to become derivative, and therefore I, too, will become derivative by default, and then the fans will say that this version of me is the worst iteration yet.

I don't even know what that means.

I do know that the one thing I *don't* want to be is boring. Anything but boring.

"I got rid of your car," I tell her.

Daneen clicks her mandibles. "That's a shame. It was such a good car, a safe car. Volvo doesn't just design their cars to pass government tests. They build their vehicles so the engine gets directed under the car in a head-on collision, instead of into the passengers' laps. That could be life or death, you know?"

I snicker. "I guess it didn't keep *you* that safe, *Duh*-neen!"

When I say her name, I say the first syllable of the word like *duh*, like you say to somebody to make them feel stupid.

"Low blow, J," she says, mandibles clicking away like triplet hi-hats in a southern rap song. She's gotten more accustomed to them in the brief time I was out abandoning her vehicle, which is something. I imagine it's hard enough getting used to being dead, nevermind the mandibles.

"I already have his personal file," I say. "Phil, I mean. He lives in Ellicott City. His wife works for Bath and Body Works. He has a young son with Werdnig-Hoffmann disease. Most of their money goes into that high-ass mortgage they got and the cost of their kid's hospital bills and alternative treatments. He drives a Prius."

Daneen frowns. "So? What's wrong with driving a Prius?"

"Nothing," I say. "I'm just telling you what kind of car he drives. You know I don't have anything against Priuses."

"Prii," she says."

"What?"

"Prii. That's what they call it when you have more than one Prius."

"Who's they?"

"Toyota. That's what they call it. And it's their car...so."

Daneen pauses between the words *car* and *so*, flicking her right maxilla out in the most condescending way imaginable. It's like an index finger bending at the third knuckle. Wiggle wiggle. Point point. It's the nanny nanny boo boo of mandibulate moves.

It's funny. With the symmetry of Daneen's face disrupted by her new mandibles, she's not as attractive as I once thought. I'm not saying she's ugly, I'm just saying she's lucky she's light skinned.

I try to keep us on point. "So back to this Phil thing."

"There's no *Phil* thing," she says. "There's just you stealing his personal information from HR and me telling you to leave him alone. What are you gonna do? Be a family annihilator? You're gonna family annihilate Phil and his family?"

"That's not what that means. That's when you kill your own family, not somebody else's."

"OK, so you're gonna annihilate Phil's family?"

I hadn't given it much thought. "I mean, yeah. I figured I would at some point."

"That's so derivative!"

"I don't know what that means!"

"It means anyone can do that. Anyone would *want* to do that. Come on, bitch, who doesn't want to kill Phil? We should be focusing on having a baby."

"A baby?" A cold eel slithers inside my lower intestines. "Why would we want a baby?"

Daneen clicks her mandibles together and stares off into the distance dreamily. "A baby is what we're missing. It would make our family complete."

"I don't think I have a job anymore. You certainly don't. And you're not in any kind of condition to do anything, really. How are we supposed to take care of a baby?"

Daneen is devastated. "You don't think I'd be a good mother?"

At this point I'm getting tired. Tired of the subject, tired physically, tired of *this*. "It's not that. I just don't think it's the right time."

"There's never a right time when it comes to something like this," she insists. "I know I'd make a great mother."

"Why do you get to be the mama?" I ask.

Daneen laughs, agitating the nearly-opaque, viscous, brown liquid in the tub. "Gosh, Jada. We can both be the mamas."

Daneen reaches out to me with a long, sinewy arm, brown water droplets coming off her forearm and elbow. She brushes my cheek with the rough pad of her decomposing index finger. I tilt my head and lift my shoulder to catch her fingers between my cheek and collarbone. I hold her hand there. Smile.

It's an intimate act, her touching my cheek then me trapping her fingers between my chin and shoulder. Like I'm holding her affectionate touch hostage.

Daneen smiles and tugs, and I ease up, releasing her hand. "I knew you'd get it," she says.

CHAPTER 36

I GET A TEXT FROM WET SYSTEMS CAR CLINIC. At this point, I have completely forgotten about them and I have to scroll back through our text message thread to remember who they are. This was the guy–I assume it was a guy–who was being a little weird. Not dangerous-weird, perhaps a little more friendly than necessary, but not in an overtly rapey way. More in an autistic kind of way. I can deal with autistic.

He texts me this:

WET SYSTEMS CAR CLINIC: I'm here at yur job

I'm confused. I don't know what he's talking about, but then I remember today is the day I am supposed to get my car cleaned. This is the day the second mobile detailer is supposed to come look at my vehicle, and we planned for him to come to Hopkins, to do it in the parking garage. I pop a Klonopin and then snap another in half between my front teeth, then swallow the half and put the other half back in my pill bottle. I have adult ADD or something, because instead of replying to the weird detail guy, I check out the newest post on Nursing Connections. It's from Charmaine HeWillNeverLeaveMe Andrews.

The post is an image of a disappointed teddy bear and the caption is: What's the worst thing that you've ever said in an interview?

The first comment is from Jakeila Bowie:

Not a nurse, but in an interview for a clinical research role I was asked to describe a time at work when I had made a mistake. I recounted the story and at the end I said, "I was such a fucking idiot." Then I gasped and said, "I can't believe I fucking said that." It was like something out of a dumb movie. My interviewer laughed and I was asked back for a second interview, though I ended up taking a different job.

And then, a bubble text message alert at the top of my screen:

???

It's from Wet Systems Car Clinic.

I text back: can you come to my apartment complex?

A moment passes. The text is green, an android, so I can't see the bubbles that let me know if he's typing or not. The next text comes through:

WET SYSTEMS CAR CLINIC: it's in the city?

I text back: no. Rosedale.

WET SYSTEMS CAR CLINIC: ard. I can do that. Text address.

Before I send him the address to Rosedale Gardens, I watch another TikTok where a woman who has gotten sober shares her redemption arc to the world.

The hashtags are: #sobertok #CNAlady #fyp

The caption below the TikTok reads: Part 1, living my best life

The video is of a woman in a hospital gown laying in a hospital bed. She holds her forearm over her forehead, her hand hanging limply. The hand shakes and the fingers feather her lifeless, dirty blonde hair. Her hair is thin, so when the fingertips move it, it looks like spider gossamer, or the fuzzy, white pappus of a dandelion.

The caption across the TikTok reads: me with 1 day clean and sober, wondering what life will be like without dr*gs

The woman has *meth-mouth*. The corners of her upper lip sink inward and turn down as a result of the lack of teeth behind them. She stares upward, at the upper right-hand corner of the camera so that she is looking away from me, as if she can't bear to look at anyone, as if she is trying to formulate some kind of plan of escape from her hospital bed.

The song that plays in the background is "Iris" by the Goo Goo Dolls.

The image in the TikTok changes to rolling footage of vivid, neon green tomato plants. Pale, yellow tomatoes hang from the stalks. More poke out from behind the leaves.

The caption across the TikTok reads: me with 5.5 years clean crying over my ripening lemon boy tomatoes

The camera pans and the woman is now in the picture, weeping and wiping tears from her eyes. Her skin looks slightly better. Her hair looks more voluminous. The skin around her mouth still looks loose and flaccid. Some things cannot be replaced or fixed as easily. Veneers are expensive. At least she can find pleasure in her lemon boy tomatoes.

The video footage switches to a still image of the woman smiling while embracing one of the tomato plants. She's really hugging on it, like she is afraid that if she lets it go it will disappear forever.

The caption across the TikTok reads: and then having a literal photoshoot with them :)

The rest of the TikTok consists of still images of this ex-drug addict posing with her tomato plants. In one of the pics, she sits next to a tomato plant with her elbow on her knee and her chin on her fist, recreating the pose of *The Thinker* sculpture.

It's giving Ariana Grande in the "God is a Woman" music video.

It's giving stupid fucking bitch.

When I think about what a stupid fucking bitch she is, I feel so empty in my stomach, like I just want to put things inside of myself until I feel like me again. I try to think about the things I like about this woman. I like how she put the asterisk in the work drugs, to decrease the likelihood of her TikTok being throttled by the algorithm. Suicide, murder, killing, drugs; they say when you type these words out on social media it limits your visibility. I like that about her. I like how she was crying with lemon boy tomato plants but still managed to do what it takes to maximize her online visibility.

I close TikTok momentarily to send the address of my apartment complex to Wet Systems Car Clinic, then open the app back up and swipe for more content.

CHAPTER 37

Sometimes I use ChatGPT to find out *what type of appliance will give you a 20(A) shock?* and *can a person survive a 20(A) shock?* and then I look around my apartment for a hand drill, or a space heater, or anything I can fuck up and intentionally create a fault in. I cover my bases by damaging the wiring *and* getting it all wet. I like to feel it in my teeth.

I felt it the first time, back when I had a job at Piercing Pagoda. I sold earrings and jewelry out of an island store in the middle of Security Square. I did the ear piercing. Just the standard places. We mostly pierced the ears of babies. Tiny, screeching things that had to be held down by their mothers. The mothers would have to wrap one arm around their baby and use the free hand of the other to bend them by the foreheads and expose their earlobes.

Then I would do my thing.

It was worse when the fathers came with the babies. They couldn't take it. Couldn't handle seeing their daughters in pain. They would wrap an arm around their child, hold the forehead with the other,

 203 

and lean back, turning their faces away and grimacing. It was unhelpful. They were practically pulling the babies away from me, making it harder to hit the target. One father leaned back so far he fell off the stool. He landed on his ass, wailing daughter in his arms clutched tight to his chest, North Face coat spread around him like a dress. He looked like a wilted flower. The whole situation was awkward for me because seeing grown men cry often results in me experiencing a vasovagal syncope episode, and he looked like he was about to cry, but also, he was a customer, so I had to just stand there and take it.

I always have to stand there and take it.

I never intentionally hurt *these* babies. I was always gentle. That's not what this is about.

The way I felt the electricity was with the ultrasonic cleaner. It's a rectangular tank made of stainless steel with a matching lid that I lost at some point somehow. The lid is to cover the tank when the jewelry is in it. The front panel has a couple buttons and a dial to adjust the time and intensity of the soak. I don't know what I did, because this was before ChatGPT, before I could ask *how did I electrocute myself with the ultrasonic cleaner at* Piercing Pagoda?

Something happened when I pulled the small tray of earrings out of the tank. My vision started clipping like I had traveled outside of the map of a video game. My teeth vibrated. Buzzed. Grinded. It was only for a moment but I felt it everywhere at once. It is the only thing I have ever felt everywhere at once.

Except hate.

Sometimes I can feel hate everywhere all at once, and much like electricity, hate is the only other feeling I can feel in my teeth. Much like electricity, my hate can create and destroy things.

Sometimes I think about my hate like *flan de leche.* I think about it like I'm being smothered in that rubbery, gelatinous Mexican mixture of sweetened condensed milk, eggs, and vanilla; baked until set and topped with caramel sauce. I feel like my mouth is being filled with the stuff. Like my nostrils are plugged with the creamy thickness. And then it's like I'm being baked and splattered with sauce. Like my car windshield. Like cum. The whole world is covered in it. It fills every crevice, every crack in me, until there's just too much of me. I can't breathe sometimes. I just have to keep swallowing. And then it's all inside of me, filling me up. I have to keep swallowing it down if I want to survive.

CHAPTER 38

I pop two Klonopin and snort the rest of the shit I got from Toussaint then wait for Wet Systems Car Clinic to arrive. The dope tastes good, like Tom Ford Tuscan Leather, but the drip gets caught in my throat. Bitumen and sand. I gulp it down and open the Youtube app on my phone. There's a red notification bell on the icon. I click on it and see there's a new short from the CurryHouseClips channel.

I click on the video and turn my phone sideways to watch it. The video begins with a low angle shot of Indiana hawthorn and blue hydrangea bushes in front of what appears to be a medical facility. The camera cuts to a POV tour of a laboratory, and we travel down a long, brightly lit hallway that turns left once, then right two times. The floor, walls, ceiling are all white, spotless.

A voiceover begins. "Our state of the art bioscience facility at the University of Maryland is a leader in the field of in vitro biology, in vivo pharmacology, discovery biologics, support drug discovery, and early development programs. Integration of these functions, together with laboratory chemistry, CMC and safety assessment, successfully deliver preclinical candidates and IND packages."

The image changes to rows of hospital beds with bodies on them. Every so often, a body moves, indicating that they are alive. Test subjects. The rows of beds stretch onward until we can no longer see them, far too many to try to count. Most of the test subjects appear to be male, although every so often I can see the shape of a woman underneath a sheet, or what appears to be a woman's shape, their long hair fanned out around their head like a halo.

I pause the video and tap the screen so that it stays illuminated.

Each test subject appears to be in some state of change. That is to say, no two subjects have the same structure or appendages. The test subject closest to the camera has more than one set of legs. His chest heaves up and down and labored wheezing can be heard. It goes on for what seems like too long. The audio of the test subject breathing without any background music or voiceover. The footage of the hospital beds and test subjects.

New frame. It's the same doctor from the last video, the scientist at the University of Maryland. "When Simone de Beauvoir wrote *The Second Sex*, Camus was salty as fuck. He got all in his feelings, said that she had disrespected the French male. Male professors refused to teach it, at best. At worst, they burned the book like right-wing religious fanatics.

Whenever we challenge them in any way, this is what they do. You have to kill them all."

Close up shot of a test subject's chest. The ribs rise up like gothic architecture. Arches flex. Something is inside. The skin pokes up, then tears. A jointed appendage bursts from the hole in the subject's chest. We hear the subject scream; can't see their face. The segmented leg unfolds and it is not a leg at all. It is a wet wing. The segmented spine snaps the membranous wing out twice. The wingspan is massive. It comes to a rest—the jointed appendage sticking up straight like an erection, the translucent wing draped over the subject and hanging off the hospital bed.

I look up from my phone and watch a black van with Wet Systems in bright red letters on the back and side, pull up in the parking lot of my apartment complex and park. My phone vibrates in my hand.

Wet Systems Car Clinic: Here

The door of the van swings open as I approach it. A large man with a pale gray complexion steps out holding a tablet. He wears a black T-shirt and black cargo pants. A black wool beanie covers his eyes.

"Nice to meet you." His voice is soft, tiny. Cartoonishly small for the body it resonates from. He swipes across the tablet screen, doesn't look at me.

"So, look." I tell him, "I've already had one place try to take care of this shit but they couldn't get it. It's like expansion foam or something. Everyone says they can get it off. But they can't."

The man looks up at me. His eyes are the color of maple syrup. And wet. "I can do it," he says.

"I hear you," I say, "but I even had one person say I would need to get the whole front of the car sanded down, buffed and repainted, the headlights replaced, new side mirrors, shit like that."

The whites of the man's eyes are milky. Something moves under the surface, like worms in deer carcasses. He repeats himself, "I can do it."

They just want a piece.

The Keloid Man's voice is *outside* my head. It's like he's right behind me. Like I can feel the sick heat of him on my neck. Through my scrubs, on my back. I turn around, and that's when I feel something split open the back of my skull. Plates shift underneath the skin, leaving me with soft spots like baby fontanelles. Everything explodes. Everything is hot and wet. Everything gapes.

CHAPTER 39

When I come to, he is pressing his thorax against me. He is a wall. A curtain. Compared to me, at my size, he is all things, no matter how hard I push. I waver in and out like a bad signal. I don't have any bars. He grabs my neck. The pads of his fingers are calloused and leave particles on me. These pieces are like grains of sand. Chalk dust. His thumbs are completely smooth. It's as if at some point his thumbs said *no*, as if his thumbs alone have lived a life of leisure while the remainder of his hands have performed decades of manual labor.

What I know is that one of my locs is caught underneath one of his smooth thumbs as he chokes me, nearly ripping it out at the root. I do feel some of the hair tear close to the scalp and think *this is bad, but I know a loctician that can reattach it for me.*

My vision gets dark in the corners, then it pin-holes completely.

Choking a person to death is more difficult than it looks.

He almost gets me there, but I wake up shortly after, curled up in a ball in the backseat of my car. My head is killing me. It's like my brain is swelling. Like my skull isn't big enough to contain it. Brain throbbing against bone, beating with my heart.

I check myself but I know already. Completely. My purse, my wallet—on the floor behind the passenger seat, everything still inside. My phone next to me, although it's been turned off, or maybe it died. I squeeze my eyes shut and press them with my palms until I see spirals and exploding stars. I am on a roller coaster. My body goes up a steep-angled incline, two thousand feet into the air. The rails and inversions are coated in black lumps. A moving void. I rise up.

The dobsonflies crawl over my face and neck. Roiling tide of chitin. Synchronized chaos. I spit with my pursed lips, tongue between them like pspst pspt pspst. The dobsonflies try to worm their way in between my lips and tongue but their bodies are too fat. I go up the incline and the roller coaster ticks. I shut my eyes. The dobsonflies try to open them with their mandibles. Twin scythes.

The carriage drops at 220 mph, reaching terminal velocity and instantly killing the dobsonflies. They pop pop pop around my head. The world moves by in a blur of gray and green. I fall and I fall until the carriage hits a flat section and torpedoes me into the first of nineteen clothoid inversions which gradually shrink in diameter. I am exposed to 10 g for one minute and 45 seconds, causing me to grayout, then blackout, then bleed from my nose and pop pop pop like the dobsonflies. The carriage makes a sharp right turn, then turns over and un-loads me into the backseat of my car and I'm back in the parking lot of my apartment complex.

When I get out of the vehicle, I see that the expansion foam cum stain shit is still there, painting the front of my vehicle like a prehistoric bird came on its face.

CHAPTER 40

MY HANDS ARE SHAKING SO IT'S DIFFICULT FOR me to open the Facebook app and get to Nursing Connections. I'm going through some things right now, so I have to cut myself some slack. Maybe I spelled it wrong, whether it's the word *nursing* or *connections*, I must have spelled one of them wrong. And that would make sense because of how stressed out I am right now. But I didn't spell it wrong. I mean, how the fuck do you spell *nursing* or *connections* wrong? You would have to be completely retarded. I am not retarded. But I can't find Nursing Connections from the Groups tab, so I type Nursing Connections in the search bar. It comes up and I click on the Group profile image and the page is private now.

A bowling ball tumbles down the lane of my chest and strikes all the pins in my ribs. The bowling ball cracks open and poison and piss and serpents pour out of it.

Restricted access.

They are trying to restrict my access.

 215 

Which means for some reason I'm no longer a member of Nursing Connections. But how could this be? This must be some kind of mistake, some kind of clerical error or administrative failure. But what if it was someone with an agenda? A group moderator who never liked me. A hater. Someone who doesn't appreciate my memes.

It's giving hating-ass bitch.

It's giving I'm going to find out who did this and kill their whole family.

I can feel the whole of my uterus and it feels like a nest of snakes inside of me. Uncoiling and coiling back in on itself. This ball of writhing snakes presses and pushes and I'm just too petite to hold it all in. The thorax ichor is all over me. It crawls over my skin, imbued with life. Spikes and horns burst from my shoulder blades. The backs of my hands look like the Keloid Man's keloids.

I need to figure out what happened. I need to get access to Nursing Connections. Immediately. I have so many memes and clever quips to post. I don't think anybody understands how important this is. Something sharp is poking the inside of my cheek and scratching around. Like it's searching for something. Inside of my mouth. I feel it slide down my throat, back to wherever it came from. This is when everything changes for me.

CHAPTER 41

PEOPLE ONLY WATCH NASCAR FOR THE CAR wrecks. I'm sure that isn't true, but regardless of whether it is or not, if you want to pay to see somebody die, look no further than the circus. You're much more likely to see the ten-year-old member of the father and son acrobat team break his neck on an awkward dismount off his father's shoulders than you are to see a car explode and burst into flames at the Richmond Raceway, and if you decide to do the circus, you don't even have to drive to Virginia. And let's be honest, who the fuck wants to drive to Virginia?

And you can get real sick with it too, if you want. I'm talking fetishizing and weird racial overtones to your accidental death voyeurism. Like, if you want to see black people die, you can get tickets to the Soul Circus. Maybe you want to see braids and faux-locs flap up in the air after somebody misses a net. The Soul Circus is at the National Harbor and there are nice shops and restaurants to check out after the show.

And if you want to see white people die, you can do Ringling Bros. and Barnum and Bailey at the Baltimore Arena. You have the opportunity to see all kinds of white death at that venue. Greek jugglers. Armenian sword swallowers. Slovenian aerialists. Israeli acrobats. Canadian tightrope walkers. Take your pick. Someone's going to die eventually.

It's not every time, but if you go enough, you'll see it. And ever since the circus stopped having animal performances—which means there's no chance you'll see a Romanian animal tamer mauled by a Bengal tiger—the ticket prices are budget friendly. Much cheaper than stupid-ass NASCAR.

The other thing about the circus: no matter what it is, they will try to add a jump rope to it. Thirty-foot tall unicycle riding around the three rings; they will throw the rider a jump rope and expect him to jump with that unicycle. Those big, metal spinning cages? The double deck wheels spinning in the air on a central axis, the performers standing on the outside of the heavy duty steel. They call them the Wheel of Death and they will add a jump rope to that shit too.

All this talk about having a baby is making me think of circuses.

The way I see it, Daneen, the baby, me; we all get tickets for the third or fourth row of the Ringling Brothers since the Soul Circus is currently in Philadelphia and we don't have the gas money. The cost of two tickets (children under three are free) is about $80 and with our shitty Hopkins salaries we can't afford much else, but somehow I still manage to scrape up $30 for an overpriced, cheap, plastic toy that lights up rainbow colors and shoots bubbles everywhere, something to wave around, to bring home—for the baby of course.

A souvenir. For her to remember the circus.

After what happened to me yesterday, I decide that my mission will be to find out if my access card for Hopkins has been restricted yet.

Underneath my scrub top, I put on an Under Armour fitted mock. The collar covers most of the bruises around my neck, and what it doesn't cover will be hidden by my hair.

When I arrive at Hopkins, I hold my card to the reader and the light blinks from red to green and I am reminded of how there is a complete communication breakdown between HR and admin and the actual healthcare workers, and they really need to do something about that.

Bureaucracy, am I right?

I swipe my card two more times to get access to the restricted areas where I clock in and put my bag away.

I run into Xiomara who reads me up and down, her lips a tight line. "I didn't think you were coming in today, honey."

"Why?" I ask.

"No reason. You just been looking a little crazy, that's all. Figure you taking some time off. To rest, you know?"

"I'm fine." My insides are nails and cutlery.

"What happened to your neck, honey?"

I focus on a spot on the wall above Xiomara's head. "Stress?"

Xiomara sucks her teeth. "I don't know, honey. You sure you OK? You don't need to go home?"

"I'm fine," I say.

Xiomara looks me in the eyes, then my lips, what I assume are the bruises on my neck, and then down to my hands. She purses her lips, then parts them slightly, seems like she is about to speak, but doesn't.

Something crawls up from the back of my throat and tickles the inside of my cheeks. It moves around behind my teeth, whatever it is. I feel it jiggle my uvula as it slips back into its hiding spot.

"You got one in 1020," she says, looking at her mobile cart computer screen. She puts her code into the system, which connects to the 'security tab on each infant's umbilical cord. She clicks the mouse and scrolls until she gets to my patient and turns off the security status of the baby being discharged.

First I pose like this for a little while:

Then I go in room 1020 and explain to the drugged
up mother how this works. I go through my speech;
the one about car seat safety, and the woman mum-
bles that she has a Graco Tranzitions 3-in-1, and holds
out a limp wrist, points to the car seat in the corner of
the room. This is great. The Graco Tranzitions 3-in-1
is one of the best, one of the safest. I explain that I
must verify that her child can be secured in the car
seat safely. I do so. The child, a girl, is sleeping, and

remains undisturbed as I strap her into the Graco. The mother tells me that her husband or babyfather or family member has brought their vehicle to the front entrance, and that he or he or they wait for me there, ready to prove that the car seat base for the Graco is installed correctly, and safely.

The walls of room 1020 are glass. I can see through them, the shifting outlines of people walking by, nurses and doctors. Shadows lap the walls like waves. Something is growing inside of me. There is a worm that wraps itself around my spine. It starts at the base and circles around. It has reached its final instar.

The mother is speaking. Her mouth moves around like lo mein and wet centipedes. Cotton fills my ears. Sunflower pattern clouds of white cover my eyes like cataracts.

The mother is speaking. I am the mother and I am speaking. Daneen says that I get to be the mama too. The shadows pass by the walls of room 1020 like fish through aquarium glass. They look like manta rays and for a moment, I want to be one too. I want to split myself from asshole to sternum and spread my ribcage skin like pectoral fins and float amongst the coral reef while smaller animals clean me.

But I can't because I'm different. I'm more than.

The last part of a child passenger safety technician's job is to ensure that the car seat is properly installed in the car they plan on leaving the hospital with, and that the dobsonfly is safe and secure in the car seat itself. We make sure the dobsonfly is strapped in the car seat while still in the room. The husband or babyfather or family member has already packed up the mother's things. Nothing remains in the room but the mother, the dobsonfly, the car seat, and myself. The mother has to leave in a wheelchair with the nurse. This is done slightly after I leave with the dobsonfly. We bring the dobsonfly outside by ourselves, to meet the husband or babyfather or family member parked in front of the hospital. There is a moment where we are with the baby dobsonfly, the fly in the car seat, no mother, no husband or babyfather or family member, just us—me, my little larvae and my car seat.

All I see is plastic and asses and titties and lips and filler and weave and lashes and acrylics and surgery and gold and Dubai and All-Star Weekend. Slick, pyretic bodies. Flesh. Meat. Shiny. Sweat and fruit and sweating fruit. They dance in the style of rub your body up and down, starting with your breasts; stick your tongue out; bend over and twerk; repeat. It's all the same dance and of course I do it too.

Instead of heading to the front, we make a right and head through the employee exit, which takes us to a skywalk which connects to the employee parking section of the Orleans Street garage. My little larvae is sleeping, completely silent, hidden beneath receiving blankets and wrapped up like a burrito.

We find our car in the parking lot and install the Graco Tranzitions 3-in-1 in the backseat, middle seat for safety. Our little one is still fast asleep. We close the door, get in the front seat.

CHAPTER 42

THE BALTIMORE SKY POURS THROUGH ME, through the bird shit cum stain splattered windshield. I drive with my dobsonfly down Orleans Street. The buildings and cars are all made of red and black speaker wire. The people I drive by also. Lengths and lengths of speaker wire wound tight and sculpted into grotesque architecture.

I take Orleans until it turns into the Pulaski Highway. I hit potholes and roll over red and black. The road writhes. It pulses. I tip the rearview mirror and stick out my tongue and it looks like a red nudibranch.

My little larvae is in the backseat. This is the first instar. It will be years before she molts.

The light up ahead is red so I slow. It's starting to rain outside. I take out my phone and check Instagram, then Facebook. When I check Facebook, I start thinking about my banishment from Nursing Connections again and consider putting the pedal to the floor and rear-ending the late model Lexus in front of me. But I hold my breath and count to five and open my eyes and see that the light is still red, so I check TikTok too, even though I'm not that into it, but I wouldn't mind seeing who's been viewing my profile since I sacrificed my own anonymity for the pursuit of having access to that feature.

I tap the icon in the upper right-hand corner that looks like light footprints to see my profile views. Men I went to school with. Women I went to school with. A lot of unknown pages without profile pics. And then Amber.

Amber.

Oh, God. Fuck yes.

The light turns green but what's this? Why would Amber be looking at *my* profile? And of course, there's an obvious reason, right? And I shouldn't get my hopes up, because if I can see that she's been view-ing my profile, it means that she can see I've been constantly viewing hers since I created my TikTok page. So why wouldn't she check my page?

But she also has thousands of followers, thou-sands of people viewing her page, why would she stop to click on mine?

The car behind me beeps and my baby dobson-fly in the backseat makes a clicking noise so I pull off through the light.

Amber checking me out is crazy. I mean, she doesn't follow me, yet, but she will. I keep checking the road. Checking my phone. It's dark out. Raining.

I click on the tiny circular image of Amber in the V.I.P. section at Euphoria that takes me to her pro-file. She's got a new video of herself at the gym doing squats and hip thrusts. She's got the phone positioned so that the camera is facing her pussy and thighs when she's recording. She dips. She presses herself outward.

A horn blares by me on my right side and an Acura blows past. My dobsonfly mewls.

I need to stay focused. For my little one. The ride from Johns Hopkins to my apartment in Rosedale Gardens is fourteen minutes without traffic. Aside from stopping at the light to enjoy the moment that was Amber, I am driving faster than normal. I can get us home.

I can't believe Amber viewed my profile. That's like one step away from her following me, which is only a few steps away from us following each other on all of our social media platforms. Well, I already follow Amber on all of her social media platforms, but soon, she will follow me and we will be on the same playing field. We should be anyway, because I'm amazing, but she doesn't know that yet, and I can't be mad at her for not knowing. She's at least as amazing as me.

Another car honks and cuts me off. I must have slowed down or swerved again. I take a look at Amber's page again. Her profile pic of her at Euphoria. The regular table for four at Euphoria is $1000. I don't even know what the eight-person V.I.P sections cost.

I jolt, eyes on the road because I almost swerved into a parked Hyundai.

That's when I see him. The Keloid Man. Raised flesh centipedes crawling around and across his bald pate. He smiles at me. He mouths the words to me.

They just want a piece.

Something. Headlights. A long, blaring horn. I wish I was live on Instagram right now. If Amber could see this she would definitely follow me. The world rotates underneath me and something enormous falls off the undercarriage of us, me and the little dobsonfly. Our dobsonfly.

CHAPTER 43

This was a terrible idea. I didn't really plan it through.

This is most likely because I have adult ADHD. I just can't see the consequences of my actions, you know?

Blood drips down my forehead and burns in my eyes. I push a molar with my tongue. Loose. I push a few more and pop one out the lower premolars on the right side, then the whole row of bottom right teeth from incisor to back molar. I spit them out like sunflower seed shells.

Somehow, I am home, although I do not know how I made it back. I'm leaning against the wall in my kitchen. I can see my serpentine sofa in the living room. It looks like an organ. I slump against the Formica countertop.

They just want a piece.

I remember the man. The Keloid Man. I saw him, yes, but something else. Him, but closer, helping me from my car.

My car?

It's gone. Completely undrivable.

They just want a piece.

There's no way he could have gotten me home. He didn't have a car. Not that I know of, at least. I've only seen him on foot. Maybe he's my angel.

I sit down on the couch. I turn on *The Whale.* It's the season finale.

Where did my little one go? I wonder.

The women are all dressed in ballroom gowns, moissanite earrings. The camera cuts away to a drone shot of the city. Punta Cana or Cancun or Panama City, I don't know, one of those. The women look ready to burst.

Red and blue lights in my window. The sounds of dogs and humans. I shake my bottle. The sound of one pill left. I pop my last Klonopin.

The camera cuts away to a close-up confessional shot of one of the contestants, this one resembling a tarsier. Her eyes are big and wet. "You know, when they said we were going to get to meet the Whale, I thought it would be one-on-one, you know? I didn't think we'd have to share him. I really shine when it's just me. I'm a disabled, neurodivergent woman of color, and certain past traumas as a result of navigating a patriarchal society where I'm constantly subjected to an endless barrage of white gazing, have made me less likely to express myself, or be outgoing. I just don't think I'll be able to compete with the other girls."

Three hard knocks on my door that I ignore.

I can feel something applying pressure to the insides of my cheeks, pressing them out. Swelling, even. Growing.

The curtain falls and all is revealed.

The Whale is God's mouth. He is a mountain of flesh. He is that which sinks an ocean. He is pink and yeasty. He is taller than dreams, wider than rational thought.

"I'M THE WHALE!" he bellows. "I'M THE WHALE!"

His voice is no longer the tinny, metallic shriek of the robot distorted vocal cords. His voice is thunder. His cries are the sound of ancient battlefields.

The Whale froths. Foamy spit-clusters the size of volleyballs form in the corners of his mouth. "I'M THE WHALE! OH GOD, FUCK! I'M THE WHALE!"

The mountain of gelatinous flesh starts to shake. The jaw of the Whale unhinges and the chin hits the dance floor with a thud. The Whale's teeth are like tombstones.

"Open up!" A man's shout from outside my apartment. Tactical flashlight beams shoot through my window at an angle from below.

"I'M THE WHALE!" the monster on my television screams. "ENTER ME, YOU MOTTLED CUNTS!"

Back to a close-up confessional shot. Same background, different girl. "When the Whale started calling us all mottled cunts, I didn't really know how to take it. Mostly because I didn't know what *mottled* meant. I looked it up though," she says, brushing away neon green hair that has fallen in her eyes, taking out her phone. She scrolls for a bit. "Mottled," she reads from the screen. "Marked with spots of different colors: having blotches of two or more colors. A mottled complexion, the bird's mottled plumage, and so on. I'm not a bird. I have a beautiful complexion. So, you can see why this is a bit of a red flag."

Dissolve transition. Shot of the contestants in their gowns. Shot of the Whale drooling, his jaw still unhinged and loose, but no longer bellowing. The Whale's jaw remains open like the gigantic clown mouth at the end of a miniature golf course, his eyes clicking left and right.

The camera pans to another confessional close-up shot, this one of the woman who looks like a pretty John Boyega. "I can see why he said the whole mottled thing about Dream. She has a lot of hyperpigmentation issues. Still, that's nothing to shame someone for. But it's the Whale, right? He's the fucking Whale. So you gotta eat that. Charge it to the game."

The camera switches to a timelapse shot of the city going from day to night. It's time to pick the winner, the lucky gal.

But the pressure in my cheeks is stretching, pushing. And then, it pops. Bursts. The skin separates, peels back. I know what they are without seeing them. I feel the shape of them.

Twin scythes.

Confessional shot. "I mean, it's not like I really have a choice," another contestant says. "It's the Whale. I mean, what the fuck? I didn't even have a passport before this. Now I'm taking trips. It's the only way I'm gonna make it out of Iowa. And I can't go back home. No way. I used my tax refund to get a plane ticket for this shit. Right before I flew out to New York for the casting call, I had to close out my bank account because a payday loan company is trying to chase me down and intercept my direct deposit. There's only one restaurant in the town I'm from and it's an Outback Steakhouse. I can't go back to serving Bloomin' Onions. I just can't do it."

A battering ram hits the door. It shakes the whole apartment. My new mandibles twitch with excitement.

The television screen blurs glitter and purple and spirals. The voiceover says, "For the season finale, we've decided to do something special. Something we've never done before. Instead of just *one* lucky contestant winning the Whale, all four of our remaining contestants will get to win!"

Pan to a close-up confessional shot of the girl that looks like a tarsier. "What the fuck? I mean, what the fuck? I put myself through all of this for *this*? For what? So I could share the win with three other bitches? The amount of trauma I've had to endure putting myself through this, it's changed me forever. Totally not worth it. I never got my one-on-one time. It isn't fair. Seriously."

Jump cut to the remaining contestants holding red roses and standing in front of the Whale.

"ENTER ME!" he roars. Puddles of pink saliva form on the floor around his chin and creep towards the heels of the contestants.

"Fuck it," says the girl who looks like a tarsier. She steps forward, climbs into the Whale's cavernous mouth, crawling over his purple tongue on her hands and knees, the red soles of her Christian Louboutins like blood under the studio lighting. The Whale gurgles, wet drowning noises, and tries to keep his mouth open. The tarsier girl crawls down his gullet—we can see her do it, the last flicker of red bottom sole slips down the black hole of the Whale's esophagus and she's gone.

The battering ram hits my door again. I hear the door frame splinter, the panko breading crunch of the wood.

The Whale screams. "NARRRRGGGHHH!" his jaw still hanging open, his mouth impossibly wide. He froths. He secretes. Orange urine pools around the mountain of ruddy flesh.

The Whale begins to shake. The umbilicals that run from his swollen neck to the apparatus behind him swing with his jerking. The Whale is the gaping mouth of God. One of the umbilicals comes loose. It snaps around like a snake, spraying the remaining contestants with fluids. Some of the girls dance under the arc of gray discharge.

They dance in the style of rub your body up and down, starting with your breasts; stick your tongue out; bend over and twerk; repeat.

Confessional shot of a contestant who is also a rapper. Her government name is *Courtney*-something but her rapper name is *Throat Goat*. Her song, "Shoot the Club Up" has over 100 million streams on Spotify and the title is a euphemism for ejaculating inside of a woman with no condom.

"First of all," she says, "I ain't worried about not a nann one of these hoes. These other hoes ain't shit for real, and they definitely ain't got shit on me, baby. Real recognize real and not a nann one of these hoes look familiar. Somebody show me to my competition. Ain't a bitch out here my competition. I'm the type of bitch to let my man use all four holes. Switch my hair up everyday so it's like he fuckin new bitches everytime I back it up. Spit on all kinds of tips and suck dick from the back. Eat all kinds of ass. Four holes, bitch. These other hoes can't keep up, feel me?"

Pan to a profile shot of the Whale. "HOLES!" he bellows. "HOLES!" His voice is like a wood chipper.

"Fuck allat," says Throat Goat, pushing the girl from Iowa out of the way and making her way to the front. "I ain't finna play with you hoes."

"And I oop, bitch!" Iowa rolls her eyes, crosses her arms. "Talk about a pick-me."

"What you say, bitch?" Throat Goat has turned around and is now walking back to confront Iowa. "I thought a broke bitch said something?"

"I just want you to get those fillers in your face dissolved and do more natural beats, bitch. It's giving old. It's giving fake. It's giving broke."

Throat Goat swings on Iowa, catching her in the side of the head, again and again, and at some point snatching Iowa's wig off, or accidentally getting the wig caught on her rings and bracelets. Iowa tries to protect her head. Throat Goat keeps swinging, the wig still attached to her hand or wrist so that each punch connects and is followed by the wig, slapping Iowa in the face and chest.

While this is happening, Dream and two of the other contestants make their way to the front. They're almost there, they can reach out with the toe of their heels and tap the Whale they're so close.

The battering ram rocks the door and I hear what sounds like muffled laughter.

Dream stands in front of the Whale and my, he is glorious in all his vacuous vastness. Just a blank canvas of hunger, an empty mouth-neck, neck-stomach. A hole to be filled. I get it now. She steps over the Whale's bottom row of teeth and before she can bring her other leg over the row with it, the Whale raises his jaw and crushes Dream between his tombstone teeth. Dream's head comes apart. The other two contestants—the ones whose names I cannot remember—are trying to push their way into the mouth, through the opening and closing rows of teeth. They lose fingers. Hands. Entire arms. The Whale is a reverse guillotine. The Whale is a magnificent retarded Hapsburg jaw.

Iowa tries to run away from Throat Goat. Her face is bloody. Throat Goat chases her. Iowa goes for the Whale's mouth and misses, diving into the side of his neck-face.

"Oh you played, bitch" screams Throat Goat, grabbing ahold of Iowa's ankle. Iowa lets out a high-pitched whine like a dying fox.

Pan to a confessional shot. Pretty John Boyega staring into my soul. "Jada, if you're watching this, pay attention."

The battering ram connects with the door once more, another crunch.

"This is it," she says. "This is the final episode. The only thing you need to worry about is hurting as many of them as you can before they stop you."

The battering ram hits the apartment door a third time. I run to the bathroom, to where Daneen is. She's all mandibles now. What remains of Old Daneen is strewn across the bathroom floor. Rags of skin, fleshy tarp. A beige kite on a zip line.

I take out my phone and go live on Instagram. Place my phone on the bathroom sink and lean it up against the mirror so that the camera gets all of this.

I throw up a peace sign at the front facing camera and say, "Hey guys, it's your girl J, and I'm about to fuck shit up!"

New Daneen crawls over the side of the bathtub, her mandibles clicking with what I assume is antici-pation. Her wings are still wet. They're translucent. Shimmering. The colors change, ripple like oceans as she flutters them lightly. First, a deep purple, then blue, then inky blackness.

"We're missing the finale, Daneen!" I cry, and now I'm actually crying.

New Daneen says, "Tktktktktktktktktktkt."

I reach out for New Daneen, embrace her. I hold her close to my body, feel her new wings flutter against my chest. Her mandibles slice into my thighs. This isn't intentional. I dip my fingers in the bloody wounds and rub the blood on New Daneen's head, between her spiny antennas. New Daneen embraces me with her six new arms and we tumble out of the bathroom and into the living room, awash with love.

The first police officer through the door takes one look at us and doesn't see the beauty in our coupling. He pulls back twice on the trigger. The first bullet travels through the wall above New Daneen's head, barely missing one of her antennas. The drywall explodes and plaster dust coats the two of us. The second shot doesn't miss. New Daneen's head explodes. Pieces of brain and chitin paint the wall behind us.

The bird shit cum stains engulf me.

I am all mandibles and knives-that-aren't-knives now. My wings are wet, my needles are ready. The deepest purple, the blue at the bottom of the Mariana Trench, and then I turn to inky blackness.

I jump-fly to the police officer and take off his face with my new mouth. I vomit up milky liquid that melts his bone structure, making him easier to get down. I slurp him up. Spit solid pieces back out onto his neck and chest. He flaps his arms up and around like he's making snow angels.

The second police officer through the door slips on vomit or blood or cum or bird shit cum and drops his gun. He lands on his stomach, putting him at eye level with me. He screams, but no sound comes out. His mouth is just a black hole and I'm staring down his throat. He scrambles for his gun, but I slash out with an unfamiliar appendage and remove his arm at the elbow. He passes out and I hear more walkie-talkies and sirens getting closer. I cock my head sideways and swing out my scythes, stretching them as far as they can go, then I snap them back at the same time like the blades of scissors, slicing through his neck and breaking his spine. Everything in my apartment, from my beautiful serpentine sofa to my beautiful New Daneen's body is lit up flashes of red and blue.

I crawl on six new legs out of my apartment. My wet wings are variegated blackness. Everything tickles my thorax. Brushing across the hardwood floor and out onto the cold cement. It feels like dust from the sun.

Another police officer stands outside the entrance to my apartment, a few steps down. When he sees me, he drops his gun and pivots in an attempt to evade me. The ankle twists and he cries out and falls to the concrete. I suck back air to scream. When I open my mouth and roar *FUCK YOU, YOU STU-PID-ASS BITCH* no words come out. Just this metal clanging sound like the inside of an MRI machine. More of that milky, gray sputum splashes the police officer in the face. It looks like bird shit cum when it hits him. He falls to the sidewalk and screams. Smoke begins to sizzle off his blistering forehead. It's simultaneously the worst and best thing I've ever smelled. I would taste it on my tongue, but I no longer have a tongue. I have a thousand tongues on every patch of retinal tissue on every lens in my compound eyes and I have no eyelids.

It's giving I will never blink again.

It's giving I can taste everything now.

The police officer has reached for his face and his hands are now stuck there; his fingertips merging with the melting flesh. He doesn't scream. He lets out this strange hissing sound as he dissolves, like slashing someone's tires. I leave him there, liquefying from the top down.

I jump-fly to the first police car I see and flip it upside down because I can. It smashes into a parked Nissan Sentra and the parking lot is filled with car alarm noises that make my mandibles ache. I wish Amber could see me now. I wish Daneen was still with me. *Where's Daneen?*

Fuck. I should be recording this but I left my phone back in the apartment. I can't go back there, I've gone too far. But I really wish I could live stream all this too. Imagining all the reactions I would get, all the likes and comments, it makes me grow. It makes me stronger.

I spring into the air and swoop down on an Amazon driver trying to get back into his delivery truck. I impale his head with both mandibles and tear it off his shoulders. I try to eat it, his head. I manage to choke down some of it, softening it with my noxious saliva. I spit out the larger chunks of skull fragments that remain solid, then kick his body to the side with my fore-legs.

A group of men are shooting dice by the green transformer box. I turn my new head towards them and wait for my vision to go thermal like the Predator from the movie *Predator* but nothing happens, nothing changes. I just see them as they are, clad in *Cashland* sweatsuits and matching Foamposites, perfect little soldiers, the same image, over and over again with my endless eyes. They're all the same. They're all the same person.

I crawl over to them faster than you would think something of my size can crawl. I kill two of them before the group can register what is happening. One of them pulls a gun out and points it at me. I stand on my hind-legs and spread my wings.

Then he actually shoots me.

The bullet travels through the lower right side of my jaw, tearing off one of my new mandibles and taking most of the right side of my face with it.

My vision changes. Disrupted. A sudden absence of visual input. Depth perception significantly compromised. Everything looks flatter. This stark reduction in visual data, disorientation. Imbalance. Warm wet runs down what's left of my face. One of my eyes is gone. I know it because I can feel the wind in my face. Not regular wind. But air that feels like wind as it enters exposed parts of me where I have never felt air inside before.

I roar and the MRI sounds come out. The energy vibrates through me. It's like when I electrocuted myself at Piercing Pagoda all over again. It hurts so bad. It feels so good. The man is covered in gray bird shit cum. He looks like a candle being made at the Amish market. In reverse. I pounce. I get my new blood all over him. I vomit up more enzymes then tear him in half with my remaining mandible. He sounds like a curtain ripping.

I hear sirens.

Fire, police, ambulance.

I can barely focus through my remaining eye now. Even with all of those tiny lenses and patches of retinal tissue. It's all red. Everything strobes. Then I see it.

The Graco Tranzitions 3-in-1 with my dobsonfly inside. Unharmed. Unblemished. Unscanthed. Perfectly perfect.

I jump-fly to where my little one is and feel my back open up. More police have arrived and they're shooting at me. Their bullets shred my new wings. Sheets of it like translucent leather fall all around me.

The car seat disappears.

My little one disappears.

I feel something leak out of me and then I feel less than. But I am so much more.

My carapace sprouts long segmented snares where my damaged wings once were. I shed the remaining wing leather. It falls like sheets. The appendages are barbed along the edges. A viscous yellow fluid drips from the tip of each limb.

I try to scream more liquid death with my broken mouth but nothing comes out. Just the sound of a transformer overloading. I look up at the milky, orange blade of sky and it glares back down at me.

I whip a scythe in the direction of the nearest officer. The segmented appendage expands at the joints until it's long enough to slice off the top half of his skull. Still alive, he cries out in bubble noises. He sounds like the end of the Keurig coffee maker cycle.

This is my moment.

This is when I know what I am, what I was always meant to be. The sun is setting on Rosedale Gardens and I am connected to everything. The roaches and the water bugs. The smell of piss and sawdust. And the Chinese sumac that grows invasively, cracking the sidewalk. I can feel it in my new appendages. I click them around me in a circle, against the broken street, feeling every pothole, every vial, every spent shell casing. The police try to break me with their bullets and I deflect as many of them as I can with my new appendages. I'll try to kill them all. As many of them as I can.

My scythes are sharp. I am beautiful. I am a beautiful inanimate object. I am knives-that-aren't-knives. I am the Challenger Deep at the bottom of the Mariana Trench. I am a sunset. The pink sky that kisses the ocean. They are mottled, I am pure.

I'll never let them take me alive.

With special thanks to

My wife, Jada, and my daughters, Juno, Halo and Rayne–you are my world.

This work is an amalgamation of the conversations and contributions of Grant Wamack, Charlene Elsby, B.R. Yeager, Ben DeVos, J. David Osborne, Kelby Losack, e rathke, Brian Allen Carr, Hobart, Matt Revert, Mike Corrao, Stephanie Kiefer, and The Johns Hopkins Birthing Center. We are the combined efforts of everyone we have ever known and I am grateful to know these people.

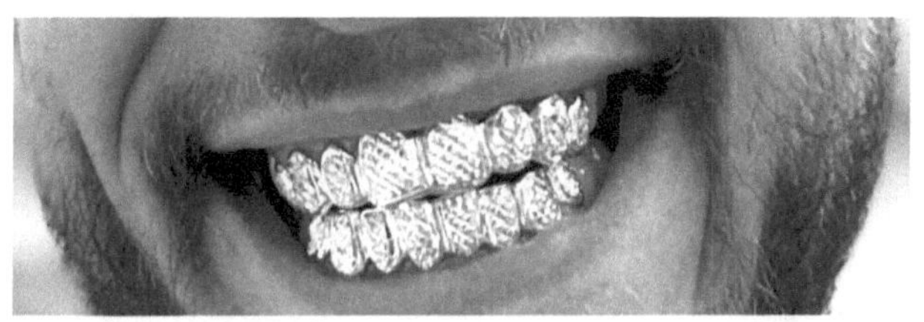

DAVID SIMMONS lives in Baltimore with his wife and three daughters. Simmons is the author of the fantastically bizarre "Ghosts of Baltimore Duology," where the supernatural and strange grapple with the ever present past of East and West Baltimore. He is a regular contributor to Books to Prisoners, a Seattle-based nonprofit organization whose mission is to foster a love of reading behind bars, encourage the pursuit of knowledge and self-empowerment, and break the cycle of recidivism.